Praise for

It's a 50/50 Thing

'This is an excellent read . . . full of suspense.' Clara, 13

'Instantly engaging' *Chicklish*

'Chris Higgins writes in a dead-on emulation of a teenage girl's voice, her prose salted with pithy observations.' *Financial Times*

'Higgins packs a lot into an easily-read book, taking the issues seriously but presenting them with a welcome lightness of touch.' *Books for Keeps*

'. . . convincingly captures the teenager's view of the world.' Julia Eccleshare, *Lovereading4kids*

'There are so many strands to this book that are beautifully interwoven.' *The Book Bag*

'Higgins us wanting

Also by Chris Higgins

32C, That's Me
A Perfect 10
Pride and Penalties
Love Ya Babe
Would You Rather?
Tapas and Tears

For older readers

He's After Me
The Day I Met Suzie

Hodder Children's Books
A division of
Hachette Children's Books
Chris Higgins
shortlisted Queen of teen
It's a 50/50 Thing

First published in Great Britain in 2008
by Hodder Children's Books
This edition published in 2013

1

A Catalogue record for this book is available from the British Library

ISBN 978 1 444 90000 2

Typeset in Bembo by Avon DataSet Ltd, Bidford on Avon, Warwickshire

Printed and bound in Great Britain by Clays Ltd, St Ives plc

The paper and board used in this paperback by Hodder Children's Books are natural recyclable products made from wood grown in sustainable forests. The manufacturing processes conform to the environmental regulations of the country of origin.

Hachette Children's Books
a division of Hachette Children's Books
338 Euston Road, London NW1 3BH
An Hachette UK Company

www.hodderchildrens.co.uk

For Vinny.

Thanks to . . .
Claire for the idea.
Charlie Tomlinson, the original Charlie T.
Jan and the St Ives School Bookgroups.
Twig, as always.

'He'll be with you in a minute, take a seat.'

The school secretary, blonde and plump, points to some plastic chairs facing each other on either side of a closed door. A sign on it says, 'Mr D. Davey, Assistant Head Teacher'. I sit down on the middle one and she gives me a plastic smile to match the chairs and clicks back to her office on her high heels.

I shift my weight and feel the chair leg wobble, and move to the one opposite. The minute stretches into five, then ten. My nervousness has dissipated and I'm getting bored. I've read the notice board with its lists of appointments for work experience but the names and placements don't mean a thing to me and there's nothing else to look at in this tucked-away corner of the school.

From a distance I can hear voices droning French verbs and somewhere a guitar is being played, badly, the same chord over and over again. A babble of voices rises suddenly, a teacher yells and the noise falls to a murmur. Familiar sounds, though quieter than my last school. I glance at the clock. I'd be in Science now. With Ella.

Tears prick my eyes and I blink furiously and stare at the school prospectus I've been given. I know it by heart already; it had been sent to me at home.

Home. No such place now. A new start, that's what Mum said. Home used to be a happy, busy place in the centre of things, Mum and Dad, me and Izzy, lots of people in and out all day long: my mates, neighbours, friends of Mum and Dad's, people involved in the skate-park . . .

'Like blinking Clapham Junction,' Dad used to say.

More like the end of the line now. The back of beyond. Just Mum, Izzy and me. No one else.

I wonder how Izzy's getting on.

There's the sound of footsteps and I sit up but it's a female teacher, past her prime, straggly greying hair, flowing skirt, all beads and bangles, you know the type. She's got someone in tow.

'Sit there, you,' she barks, 'and don't move.'

A tall, long-limbed boy with scruffy dark hair sprawls on to the chair I've vacated, the one with the wobbly leg. There's an ominous crack and the boy and the chair end up on the floor. The woman looks outraged, as if he's done it on purpose.

'Get up!' she snaps. 'Now you're for it. You wait till Mr Davey sees what you've done.'

The boy unfolds himself from the floor and stands up slowly, dusting himself down. His trousers are low-slung and baggy under his school shirt. 'Wasn't my fault,' he says casually. The woman raps on the door, rigid with rage. I could have told her there was no one in. If she'd asked.

'What's going on?' Behind us a man appears, tall and clean-shaven, dressed in an open-neck shirt and light trousers. Next to the woman he looks cool and calm and not-to-be-messed-with.

'Mr Davey, I will not have this boy in my Year 10 class any more. He's insolent, he's disruptive and he won't listen to a word I say . . .' Her face is red with indignation and her chest heaves as she spews out a catalogue of complaints. The boy stands by silently, an expression of faint amusement on his face, and I can see that even D. Davey himself is finding it hard to stifle a yawn. 'And now look what he's done!' She indicates the broken chair in triumph, a shattered symbol of all his transgressions, and Mr Davey raises his eyebrows, impressed despite himself.

'Destroying school property, Jermaine? That's a new one, even for you. An exclusion offence on its own.'

The boy shrugs. He doesn't care, you can tell. But I do.

'It was broken already.'

Three surprised pairs of eyes turn their attention to me. I feel my colour rising but I keep on anyway. It's not fair, his getting the blame for something he couldn't help. I hate miscarriages of justice.

'The leg was wobbling when I sat on it.'

'Did you do it?' The teacher turns her spleen on me.

'No! I moved so *I* didn't end up on the floor.'

The boy smiles lazily. 'Yeah, it's dead dangerous that. I could have broken my neck.'

'No such luck,' mutters Mr Davey. 'Who are you, by the way?'

'Kathryn O'Connor. I'm new.'

'Kathryn,' says Mr Davey thoughtfully. I can see his mind ticking over and I know he's been fully briefed. 'Welcome to Stanford Technology College. STC for short. It's OK, Mrs Walker, I'll deal with Jermaine.'

Mrs Walker looks me up and down with dislike then gives Jermaine one last sweeping glance of venom and stalks off down the corridor, back still taut with anger. Jermaine's upper lip curls in contempt. It's very attractive but Mr Davey doesn't think so.

'Sit down and wipe that smirk off your face. I'll deal with you in a minute. Kathryn, into my office please.'

Jermaine makes a sardonic sound in his throat, but his face is impassive. I pick up my bag and go to step over his outstretched legs and I notice suddenly that his shoe is worn down on the left toe. My eyes move up to his face with renewed interest and he pulls back his legs and says, 'Sorry.' When he smiles, his eyes crinkle appealingly.

In the office Mr Davey indicates a chair and rummages through his filing cabinet. He pulls out a folder. 'Here we are, Kathryn O'Connor.' I can see a piece of paper with the letterhead of my old school on it and I wonder what they've written about me. He starts filling in a form. 'What do you want to be known as?'

'Sorry?' Does he think I'm going under an assumed name? On reflection, that might be a good idea.

'Do you like to be called Kathryn? Kathy? Kate?'

He makes it sound as if I can choose. New name, new identity. I hear myself saying,

'Kally. I'd like to be known as Kally.'

'Kally with a K?' I nod. He crosses out my Christian name and prints 'KALLY' in capital letters.

Why did I say that? That's not what he meant at all. When Izzy was little she couldn't manage Kathryn and she used to call me Kally, but I hadn't been called that for years. Too late, it was done now and I couldn't go back without making myself look a complete idiot. I run through the rest of the form with him then he sits back and looks at me, tapping his teeth with his pen.

‘I know things have been hard for you, Kally, but nobody except for the Head and myself is aware of what’s happened. And that’s the way it’ll stay. In the meantime if you need to talk you know where to find me. My door is always open.’

Hardly.

‘In a manner of speaking, that is.’ He’d read my thoughts. My mouth twitches and he winks at me. He’s nice. He gets up to open the door. ‘You’ll settle in well, I’m sure. We’re a friendly lot.’

Outside, the boy is sitting with his legs up on the chair opposite. Mr Davey sweeps past, knocking them to the ground. ‘Most of us are, anyway,’ he amends. ‘Come with me and I’ll show you to your classroom. Don’t move an inch, Jermaine.’

‘Great hair,’ the boy says to me. I smile back then hurry to keep pace with Mr Davey.

‘Watch him,’ says the teacher shortly. ‘He’s trouble.’ I follow him down the corridor, through reception and up the stairs, passing lots of classrooms on the way. I glance through the windows but it’s all a bit of a blur, though the general impression I get is that it’s all fairly quiet with no one causing a riot. No one except Jermaine obviously.

We stop outside a classroom and Mr Davey raps on the door. Inside it’s silent, they’re writing furiously, but twenty-odd pairs of eyes look up to inspect me with interest as I follow him in. The teacher is marking a pile of books. She's young and pretty.

'Nice and quiet in here, Miss Johnson!'

'They're doing a test.' She smiles at us both.

'Kally O'Connor, new girl.'

I'm being scrutinized from head to toe by the whole class. They notice my hair first, everyone does, you can't miss it, it's thick, red and wiry with a mind of its own, though it's on its best behaviour today because I've yanked it back into a ponytail for school.

Eyes move to my face next. How do you describe your own face? Blue eyes inherited from both parents but with Dad's dark lashes, thank goodness, Mum's pale, transparent skin, my own chiselled nose with annoying freckles on it and a small chin that Dad calls determined.

Called.

They're all staring. I can sense them eyeing up my figure now. I bet they can read my thoughts. I feel like I've been splayed against a screen and X-rayed. Stay cool.

A boy at the back nudges the one beside him and despite myself I can feel my heart beating faster and my colour rising, one of the disadvantages of having the fair skin that goes with red hair, and suddenly I have a blind moment of panic when I think I'm going to turn and run, straight out of the classroom and as far away from this strange new school as I can.

Then the teacher smiles and says, 'Hello, Kally, pleased to meet you,' and a girl near the front says, 'She can sit here, Miss,' and I sling my bag on her table and sink gratefully into the chair next to her. 'French test,' she mouths and starts scribbling again, her hand under her fringe keeping stray wisps of hair out of her eyes.

'Five minutes to go,' says Miss Johnson and everyone gets back to their work. My heart slows down to normal pace and I look around. It's a big, airy room with displays of work on the wall and posters advertising French life. The tables are set out in rows, two to each table, and along one wall is a row of computers. It's tidy and workmanlike and safe. I feel myself relaxing.

When the bell goes, Miss Johnson collects the papers, then comes over to talk to me.

'Have you done French before, Kally?'

I nod. 'Since Year 7.'

'Good. I'm just in the process of setting for next year. You might like to take this test home tonight and give it a go. It'll help me assess which group to put you in.'

I take the paper and put it in my bag. A voice says, 'That's not fair, Miss. She could get her mum or dad to help her. We had to do it in class like an exam.' It's the boy who was sitting at the back, the one who nudged his sidekick. He's got a shaved head and his eyes are small and close together. He looks like a pig and I decide instantly that I hate him.

I'm not the only one apparently. The girl next to me says, 'Shut it, Darren. What's it to you?'

Miss Johnson intervenes. 'It's not the only method of assessment and Megan's right, it's nothing to do with you, Darren. Now, Kally, you'll need an exercise book and this is the textbook we use . . .'

By the time she's finished explaining everything my head's reeling and I wonder how I'm going to find my way to my next lesson, but outside the classroom Megan's waiting for me. I appraise her suspiciously. Is she one of those sad kids without a friend who's hoping to latch on to the new girl?

She doesn't look sad. She looks cool. She's got long hair that spills down her back in a blonde waterfall. Lucky thing. Mine would never do that, even if I straightened it to within an inch of its life; it's got a fiery, wiry, spirally mind of its own.

She's also tall and slim and her skirt is hitched up to show off her long, tanned legs.

I should hate her, but I don't. I like the look of her, despite the fact she's gorgeous, because she obviously does not, unlike nearly every other girl in the class, slavishly follow The Must Have, This Season, So Hot Style Secrets from the pages of the latest fashion magazine. Like my hair, she looks as if she has a mind of her own.

'Ready? We've got English next. Whingy Walker.'

My heart sinks. 'Mrs Walker? I've met her already.'

Megan wrinkles her nose. 'She's a dag.'

I follow Megan along the corridor and decide to take a risk.

'Megan?'

'What?'

'Do you know what a dag is?'

She turns to look at me and says, 'No, what is it?'

'It's the horrible, woolly, dirty bit that hangs off a sheep's bottom.'

She pauses. I hold my breath.

'How do you know that?'

'I watch *Neighbours*.'

Does she think I'm a know-all? Does she think I'm weird? She sniffs.

'Well, you learn something new every day.' Then she grins. 'Like I say, she's a dag.'

We both burst out laughing and when we get to English late and Mrs Walker glares at me and says, 'NOT a good beginning, you're late,' and Megan mouths 'Dag' at me over her shoulder, I don't worry about being new and being on public display any more, I'm just trying my best not to laugh.

Izzy's sitting on the front doorstep waiting for me when I get home. She's got all her Barbies out and she's operating on them. Heads, arms and legs are lined up on the granite step, waiting to be transplanted on to the assembled nude bodies. She's obsessed by all things medical. It looks as if she's just performed her first gender realignment surgery as Ken's head is repositioned on a torso which sports a monumental pair of breasts. He looks very pleased with himself.

'Izzy-Wizzy, let's get busy!' I dump my bag on the path and squat down on the step beside her. 'I'll get them dressed for you while you finish operating.' I select a particularly fetching little pink number for Ken which shows off his new shapely legs to perfection. He deserves it after what he's been through.

'Is that you, Kathryn?'

Like, who else would it be? No one knows us in this

back-of-beyond place. Which is precisely why we're living here.

'Yes, Mum.' I'm concentrating on shoving Ken's arm through a minuscule sleeve. That's it. I Velcro him speedily up the back to protect his modesty from my mother's prying eyes. I can feel her hovering behind me in the doorway. Hovering, not hoovering. She does a lot of the former and not so much of the latter nowadays. She sighs heavily when she sees the array of body parts. She sighs a lot nowadays too.

'Don't encourage her. Why can't you play with them nicely, Izzy?'

'I'm not playing, I'm performing a procedure,' mumbles Izzy who stays up watching hospital dramas when she can get away with it and knows all the jargon. She's tucked an amputated leg between her lips for safe-keeping while she struggles to stretch the socket she's trying to insert it into, so the sophistication of her vocabulary is somewhat marred by her indistinct delivery.

Still, she's ace for a six-year-old. She keeps me sane now I spend so much time with my mother. She's like a buffer between us, making sure we don't collide too often.

'How was school?'

'All right.'

'Is it like Deanswood?'

'No.'

How could it be? I knew everyone at Deanswood, I'd been there for nearly three years and had been at primary school before that with most of them. I knew all the places you could go if you wanted to snog someone or have a fag or miss a lesson, not that I did any of these things. I knew the people who were cool and the people to avoid like the plague and I had loads of mates.

Had loads of mates. Past tense.

'Not too bad though?'

Stop keeping on! I know what she's doing, she just wants reassurance that everything's all right, that I'm happy, that she's done the right thing moving us lock, stock and barrel away from prying eyes and caustic tongues to this remote part of the country where nobody knows us and we can start again. Well, I'm not playing her game.

'They've registered me as Kally,' I say and wait for the reaction.

'Kally!' says Izzy approvingly. 'Fab!'

'Good idea,' says Mum.

'Why?' I challenge her though I know exactly what she means. It's what I was thinking. New name, new me.

'Makes a change,' she says limply. 'A change is as good as a rest, so they say.'

Yeah, Mum, right. In that case we must be the most

rested family in Britain, the changes we've undergone in the past year.

But we're not. We're the most uptight, jittery, stressed-out threesome on the planet. No, twosome. Izzy's OK, if you don't count her obsession with body parts.

But she does keep asking when Dad's coming back.

Today though, she's got her new school to talk about. She chatters on over tea, about her fab new teacher, Miss Baker, and her fab new friend, Molly Moulton. Fab's her new word. She talks about Molly as if she's known her for years. All thoughts of her previous friends have vanished. Lucky thing. I envy her selective memory.

'Molly says I can go and play on Saturday. Can I, Mum? She's got a dog and a rabbit and her brother's got stick insects. Can we have a dog, Mum?'

'I don't know . . .'

Mum's considering the first question, I can tell by the worried frown that's appeared between her eyebrows. It's never far away nowadays. Izzy thinks she's answering the second. Her eyes brighten and she sits up straight, her voice rising an octave in excitement.

'Please, Mum. I'll look after it. I'll take it for walks and I'll feed it and bath it and it can sleep on my bed. Ple-ease!'

'No!' Mum snaps and Izzy visibly deflates.

'Why not?' I ask, but I know the answer already. A dog's too visible, it bounds about and barks and attracts attention. People might notice you.

'You couldn't look after it, you're at school all day.'

'*You* could,' I say but when I glance up at Mum I feel mean. She's tired and thin and strained and only just about holding together enough to look after us.

'We can't afford a dog,' she says. 'Anyway, we haven't got the room for anything else. It's a tight enough squeeze just for the three of us.'

Mum's right. It's a tiny two-up, two-down cottage with flagstones on the floor and exposed black timbers that are so low I can reach up and touch them. Upstairs, Izzy and I share Mum and Dad's double bed in a room where the roof comes down sharply on one side to a small window that looks on to the front garden which is wild and overgrown. Mum's squashed into a boxroom behind us in my old single bed. Downstairs there's a kitchen at the back with no cupboards, just open shelves, so everything we eat and drink is on display for everyone to see, not that anyone comes, and a small sitting room at the front with an open fire that we haven't used yet. A tiny bathroom with toilet, washbasin and ancient cracked enamel bath that you couldn't swing the proverbial cat in completes all the mod-cons.

Why would you want to do that? Swing a cat, I mean.

'She's got a point, Izzy. There's only just room enough for us.'

Mum looks at me gratefully. I don't usually stick up for her. It's not that I blame her for what's happened, it was nothing to do with her, it's just that I hate the way she's handled it all. It makes me feel guilty, all this running away and hiding, as if *we* did something wrong.

Izzy relapses into silence. She wouldn't have done that before, she would have argued and cried and tossed her hair and kept on till she got her own way, but now she knows there's no point. It was Dad she could twist around her little finger, not Mum.

I get my books out and get down to the little homework I've been given, the French test and ten sentences on My Hero for Whingy Walker. Ten sentences! I hate teachers being prescriptive like that. What if I wanted to write an essay? Or a whole book? She's only saying ten sentences so she doesn't have too much to mark.

Lazy cow.

No, I take that back. Stop being so horrible, Kally, you never used to be like this when you were Kathryn.

The French test is easy, nothing I haven't encountered before, and certainly nothing I would need help on. What was the name of that creep who said I would cheat? Darren. Hopefully he'd be in a different set next year. Bottom set probably. Lucky for me not all the boys at STC were like him. Now Jermaine, he was a different kettle of fish altogether.

He said he liked my hair.

I liked his too. Long and dark with a heavy fringe that he kept sweeping out of his eyes.

Dark eyes too. With thick dark lashes.

Dark Boy.

There was no one like him at my last school.

I suddenly realize I've doodled a kettle with a pile of fish heads poking out of it on the corner of my French test. I add long eyelashes to their fish eyes. Cute! I giggle aloud. Mum looks up at me in surprise. She's sitting in front of the empty fireplace sewing name tapes on Izzy's PE kit. She smiles too.

'It's going to be all right, isn't it, Kath?'

Reassurance again. When did I turn into the mum?

It's the first time she's smiled for months. I take a deep breath.

''Course it is. And it's Kally now. Remember?'

'Kally?' She nodded. 'Kally it is.'

I finish my homework, scribbling down the required ten sentences about my hero. I choose Charlie T, a skate pro who's big in the States. He's a big beast of a guy with feet like a dancer's who has the ability to make the most difficult moves look easy. I've got all his videos and I reckon I know enough about him to write a book if I wanted. But I'm cheating. He's not really my hero.

My hero was Dad.

When I go up to bed I think Izzy's fast asleep at first but as soon as I get into bed I can feel her hot little body tense and alert beside me. She's lying on her back feigning sleep but when I say, 'Izzy?' she turns and stares at me.

'Kath?' she says and then stops.

'It's Kally again now. Remember how you used to call me that when you were little?'

She nods. Her eyes are huge and solemn in the moonlight.

'What's up?'

A tear wells up in the corner of her eye and splashes down on to the pillow. I put my arm round her and cuddle her. Her body is stiff and unyielding.

'What's wrong, Iz-Wiz?' Suddenly she bursts into tears and there's no stopping her. I hold her close to muffle her cries so Mum won't hear her. She wouldn't be able to handle this. I can feel a damp patch growing on my pyjama top and I hope it's tears, not snot. At last Izzy stops sobbing and goes into sniffing and hiccuping mode. Finally I dare to say,

'What was all that about? Is it because you want a dog?'

'No, silly,' she says and her voice catches on another sob. 'Silly Kally.'

'OK!' Don't get annoyed, Kally, she's only little. Try to understand. 'Is it your new school? I know, I feel strange too but we'll get used to it. It'll be all right, Iz.' Who am I trying to convince?

'I like school. I like Molly, I told you.' She glares at me. Her nose is running and she catches it with her tongue. Gross.

Now my patience is wearing thin. My damp pyjama top is clinging to my skin and it's nasty and uncomfortable and feels suspiciously like mucus. I pluck a tissue out of the box beside the bed and scrub my top then thrust another one into her hand.

'Here! Blow your nose!'

Her tears well up again at my tone and she wails, 'I want Dad!'

I swallow hard. Izzy's been so good since Dad's gone. It's Mum and I who do the crying over Dad. In private of course and never together. You see, we know what we've lost; Izzy just thinks he's away from home, working.

It was something I'd disagreed with Mum about, all this pretence. I thought she should have told Izzy what had happened. But Mum said she was too young to understand.

'What's age got to do with it?' I'd yelled. 'I'm grown

up and I don't understand!'

'Neither do I,' she'd said, white-faced.

'Sshh!' I say in desperation as Izzy's howls increase. 'Mum will hear you!'

As if on cue, Mum's voice floats up the stairs, high-pitched and reedy with anxiety. 'What's going on up there? What are you two up to?'

'Izzy had a bad dream! She's OK now!' I hear the door of the sitting room closing again and I hiss at my distraught little sister, 'Shut up, Iz! You'll upset Mum!'

Obediently, Izzy turns over and buries her face in her pillow, her small body convulsing with smothered sobs. Even in her distress she knows, instinctively, Mum must be looked after. It's heartbreaking. I stroke her hair gently.

'Stop crying, Iz. He'll be back one day.'

'No, he won't.'

'Of course he will!'

She raises her face and glares at me through swollen, accusing eyes. 'He won't, Kally. You said so yourself.'

'I didn't!'

'You did!' She shudders. 'There's no room here, you said. There's just enough room for the three of us. So he can't come back, can he?'

The next day she's back to normal, up with the sun while I'm still mouldering in the bowels of my bed, unwilling to face the day. I can hear her chatting away happily to Mum in the room below, her voice floating up between the cracks in the floorboards. Mum's stained them and put motley-coloured rugs down around the house instead of carpets in a vain attempt to brighten the place up. It does nothing for the acoustics or privacy either.

I'm surprised we got away without Mum coming up to investigate what was going on last night. It's as if she's only half awake, nowadays. She's got into the habit of having a drink and dozing in the chair before she goes up so she can fall straight into bed and oblivion. She calls it a nightcap.

I'm amazed at my little sister's capacity for recovery. I think her method is brilliant. Pass your worry on to someone else and forget about it.

That someone else being me. So *I* comfort her and convince her that Dad will be back with us one day, *she* falls asleep happy, and *I* lie there awake worrying all night long, listening to her soft little snuffles and contented sleep noises.

You see, until last night, maybe I'd been under the same delusion as Izzy. Though my head tells me otherwise, in my heart I believed that Dad was coming home one day. It would only be a matter of time before he'd open that shabby front door and walk straight in and say, 'Blimey, Jan, this place could do with a lick of paint,' and get his brush out and make everything as good as new.

Steve and Jan.

Spick and span.

Everything perfect again.

Only it would take more than a lick of paint to put things right in this family.

I turn over and bury my face in the pillow with a groan as my mother calls up the stairs,

'Come on, Kally, you don't want to be late for school.'

'Don't I?' I mumble, but I sweep the duvet back and clamber out of bed. The bus leaves at the end of the lane in ten minutes and if I miss that it's a good half-hour walk and I'll be late and I'll get it in the neck from Whingy Walker because, guess what? She's my form tutor as well as my English teacher. Great.

I make it, just. The bus is pulling away but I hammer on the doors and the driver begrudgingly opens them, grumbling away as I smile sweetly and flash my pass at him. Misery-guts. There are some smokers at the back and I recognize faces from my year and a girl with long hair waves to me so, though I don't smoke, I wonder if I dare go up and join them. Then I see Piggy Darren among them and I change my mind and sit down suddenly halfway along with the younger kids and I can hear the smokers laughing and I bet they're talking about me, so I stare out of the window and wish I was having a laugh on my old school bus with my old mates, only that's not going to happen, is it?

I'm so locked into my own gloom that I don't even notice Jermaine getting on the bus till he flops down next to me.

'Don't mind, do you?' he says, dropping his bag on the seat in front. It's got skateboard straps on it and so now he gets my full attention. 'Only I can't stand cigarette smoke and I need some intelligent conversation before I tune out for the day.'

'How do you know I'm intelligent?'

'I can tell. You're your own person. I like that.' He grins at me and I feel absurdly pleased. 'It's Kathryn, isn't it?'

'Kally,' I say quickly. 'Kally O'Connor.'

'Jermaine Smith. You can call me Jem. We've got a lot in common, you know.'

'Have we?'

'Oh yes. We're both new for a start. You're the new girl, I'm the new boy.'

He's surprised me and he knows it.

'You thought I'd been here for ages, didn't you?'

'Yeah, I just assumed . . .'

'Don't. Assume, that is. "Assume makes an ass of u and me." Get it?'

I stare at him blankly then my brain kicks into gear and I laugh.

'Whingy Walker! She said that in our English lesson yesterday!'

He clicks his fingers and points at me. 'You got it. She says it all the time. See, I knew you were intelligent.' He smiles and my stomach does a kick-flip. He's so good-looking.

'No, I've only been here a month,' he continues. 'That's why I've still got a brain. Be careful, they disappear quickly at STC. You've got to keep your wits about you, otherwise they shrivel up and die and before you know it you've become a moron.'

From the back seat Darren's voice can be heard telling a joke. It's crude and involves a lot of foul language. His cronies laugh uproariously at the punchline.

'See what I mean?' Jem swivels round in his seat to face the crowd at the back of the bus and raises his eyebrows. Gradually they all fall silent. When he has everyone's attention he says in a quiet, reasonable tone, 'There are ladies present. And children.'

'We're just messing,' mumbles Darren.

'Well, don't,' says Jem. His voice is perfectly pleasant and polite, but a chill goes through me. Jem is amazing, he has such presence. Most teachers couldn't control a mob like that and he can only be a year or two older than them; he's in Mrs Walker's Year 10 English group. I almost feel sorry for Darren. Jem turns back to me and winks.

'Morons,' he repeats and I laugh out loud but then wish I hadn't because the bus is silent and everyone is listening. It pulls up outside the school gates and he stands up to let me pass.

'See you later,' I say, swinging my bag on to my shoulder.

'Absolutely,' he says and I feel a thrill run through my veins. As I step off the bus he calls, 'Kally?' and when I turn he takes a photo of me on his phone.

'Thanks,' he grins. I grin back. Jem is something else.

I have to go to the office first to sort out school dinners and there's a queue, so by the time I find my way to my classroom for registration everyone's already there in small packs chatting and my heart sinks. Then Megan disengages herself from the biggest group of girls and calls, 'Over here, Kally,' and I go and join her gratefully and she says, 'What's this about you and Jem?' and I recognize the girl with long thin mousy hair and a round face who was on the back seat.

'What about Jem?'

'I hear he was chatting you up on the bus,' Megan says and I glance at the girl and she flushes so I take heart.

'We were talking. He wasn't chatting me up. Problem?'

'Holly fancies him,' says Megan and the girl squeals.

'No, I don't!'

'Yes, you do,' says Megan, 'and so do most of the girls in the school.'

'Including you?' I ask.

'No. Not me.' She eyes me steadily. 'Not my type.'

'That's all right then. What have we got first?'

It turns out it's double English. We all have to read out our ten sentences for Mrs Walker; I can't believe it, it's like primary school. She's not even going to bother to mark them so I have to sit through twenty-odd versions of Year 9 heroes and heroines, most of whom have stepped straight off the pages of celebrity magazines, premier division clubs or the latest TV reality show. There are some good ones though.

Darren's, funnily enough. He talks about his uncle who was a young soldier in the Falklands War. And it's not the standard soldier-hero type of thing, it's sad really. He was caught up in an attack and knocked unconscious. He came round to find his mates had been killed and he panicked and ran away to hide. When they found him he was discharged in disgrace and he's never got over it to this day.

'They said he was a coward,' ended Darren. 'But to me he's a hero. He still suffers from post-traumatic stress disorder after all these years and it's really hard, but he tries to get on with his life and he never complains.'

Mrs Walker looks surprised and says, 'Well done, Darren,' and I decide he's not so bad after all until it's my turn and I read out my ten sentences on Charlie T and there's a silence, then Darren goes, 'Bor-ing!'

Thanks, Pig-Face.

There are some other worthy ones about people like Mother Teresa and Nelson Mandela and the fire-fighters at the Twin Towers (what, all of them?) but it's Megan's that really stands out. She talks about her dad and how he's her hero because he's brought her up on his own since her mum died and how he holds down an important job but he's always there for her, and it's obvious that she loves him to bits and I'm really jealous of her even though her mum's dead. At the end I've got a lump in my throat and so has everyone else because there's a silence and then everyone starts clapping and someone yells, 'Go, Mr Davey!' and they all cheer.

I look at Megan in surprise because I didn't realize Mr Davey was her dad. I'm even more jealous of her now because she's got a dad who's popular and respected, just like my dad was, and I should have had the courage to write about him but I didn't.

And then it hits me that she's only been friendly towards me because Mr Davey told her to.

So I sit there hating myself and Megan and everyone else, under a black cloud of misery which gets bigger and heavier till it threatens to suffocate me, and when the bell finally goes for break and Megan says, 'Coming?' I practically snarl, 'No!' She's taken aback and I add, 'I'll catch you up,' but by that time the damage is done and she turns away, saying, 'Suit yourself,' and goes off with Holly.

Then I'm left on my own, serves me right, and I feel so miserable I want to run away but there's nowhere to run to.

Suddenly I'm totally overwhelmed by it all and I can't hold it together any longer.

And that's when Jem comes in and rescues me.

'Kally?'

I've got my head down on the desk wallowing in my own misery when I feel a hand on my shoulder and I realize I'm no longer alone. I look up, watery eyes, runny nose, blotchy face (like Izzy I can never cry prettily), to see Jem perched on my desk, concern etched into those amazing brown eyes.

'I need a hanky,' I mumble. He roots around in his pockets and shakes his head. Then, do you know what he does? He bows his head and grasps his left sleeve between his teeth and tears the cuff off his white school shirt with his right hand. I gasp.

'What did you do that for?'

'You. Come here, snotty.' He wipes the tears from my eyes and my cheeks then he puts the cuff to my nose. 'Blow.'

I do so obediently. I feel like Izzy, six years old again,

and it's a nice feeling but I grab the material quickly out of his hands in case there's anything horrible in it and then wonder what to do with it.

'Bin it,' he says, reading my mind. 'I don't want it back.'

'What will your mum say?'

'Nothing,' he says shortly. 'You OK now?'

I nod and smile at him weakly. 'Thanks.'

'Want to talk about it?'

He's so nice. So much more grown up than anyone else. Suddenly I want to talk, tell him everything.

'It's my dad.'

Tears threaten me again. He leans forward and gently wipes a stray one from my cheek.

'Is he ill? Dying? He's not dead, is he?'

I shake my head.

'Has he walked out on you? That's a bummer. Mine did too.' His eyes are sad.

I shake my head again. How can I explain? If I tell him I'm crying because I wished I was brave enough to do my English homework on my dad and read it out to the class, he'll think I'm mad. But anyway, I'm not allowed to tell him the truth. We've got a story I'm supposed to keep to.

'He's working away. Abroad. I miss him.'

'Is that all? Well, he'll be back one day.' He draws back and glances at the clock. The bell's about to go. He thinks

I'm stupid, I know he does, he thinks I'm making a fuss about nothing. He gets off the desk and I panic. I want to feel his hand on my cheek again. I want him to care.

'It's not that simple . . . I don't know when he'll come back, *if* he'll come back!' My voice rises in agitation. He stops, seeing my distress. 'It's complicated . . .' My words tail away. Don't say too much, Kally. That's why we moved down here, remember. Don't give the game away.

The bell goes and almost instantaneously people start pouring into the classroom, glancing curiously at Jem and me. Saved by the bell. I open my bag to check my timetable, aware that Jem is still standing there watching me.

'We'll talk about this later,' he says. 'After school?'

I nod. He turns and goes out of the classroom, holding the door open for Megan as he leaves. Her eyes move from him to me.

'You OK?' she asks.

I nod. 'Fine.'

She looks as if she's going to say something but changes her mind and picks up her bag. 'Maths next,' she says. 'Follow me.'

The day passes in a blur. Lessons are no problem, I'm well up on most of the stuff they're doing. STC seems a bit more chilled-out than Deanswood, the pace is that much slower. I even get a handle on science and maths, my two least favourite subjects. At lunchtime Megan offers to take me to the canteen which is pretty nice of her considering the way I cold-shouldered her at breaktime. I pay for a packet of insipid-looking sandwiches and a bottle of water, resolving to bring my own lunch from now on.

'Follow me,' she says and leads me towards a table where Holly and some other girls from my class are congregated.

Then I notice the shoes, left foot scuffed on the toe, laces snapped and knotted up again. Jem. He's at a table on his own with his back to me, legs sprawled out in the aisle, just asking to trip up someone with a laden tray. Even from the back he looks cool. Too cool for school.

He glances up as I pass him and I say, 'Hi,' and his face lights up in a lazy smile and I hesitate, wondering if I should sit next to him. He moves his legs as if to say, 'Yeah, join me,' and I'm about to. But then Megan calls, 'Over here, Kally,' and I can't blank her again, so I smile back and say, 'See you later,' and for a minute he looks startled and then I move on and the moment is past.

And I wonder if I imagined it all until I sit down at the girls' table and Holly breathes, 'I can't believe you blew Jem out!' and I say, 'I didn't. I just wanted to sit with you lot.' Megan smiles and says, 'Good on you, girl,' and I'm glad I made the right choice because everyone's more friendly now, asking me loads of questions about my last school and my family and why I moved here.

I remember to keep to the planned story.

I tell them my dad works abroad and my mum fancied a change of scenery and then I ask them about themselves. You see, I've learnt that's the best way to get attention away from you. People love to talk about themselves, unless they've got a secret, that is. Actually, it's nice to chat about girly stuff again, finding out what people like doing and who likes who, and I suddenly realize, for the first time in ages, I'm enjoying myself.

That is, until I glance up and I notice Jem has gone. I feel a pang of regret then. It would have been nice to talk to him too. Never mind, I'll see him after school.

Only I don't.

When school's over Megan says, 'We're going round town. Want to come?' and I'd love to but I want to see Jem so I say, 'No, I've got to get home.' For some reason I don't want her to know I'm meeting Jem. I don't know why, something to do with the way she said, 'He's not my type,' or maybe because her dad said he's trouble. I watch her going off arm in arm with Holly then I hang about the bus stop waiting, letting one bus go after another, but there's no sign of him. He's stood me up. I bite my lip and sigh deeply. Well, let's face it, it wasn't exactly a date, was it?

In the end I jump on a bus but it's the wrong one and then I have to get two because I'm miles out of my way and by the time I get home Mum's in a strop and has a go at me and I'm really fed up. Try eating dried-up macaroni cheese for tea with no one for company but a middle-aged depressive and a manic six-year-old when you've screwed up a friendship with the only interesting male in the school before it even started and you'll see what I mean.

I go up to bed early because there's nothing on the telly and I don't feel like being cross-examined by Mum about my day just because nothing remotely exciting has happened in hers. Izzy is stretched across the bed, dead to the world, mouth open, arms flung wide. I don't even have a bed to myself.

I wonder how much more of this I can stand.

You see, the worst thing is, I've got no one to talk to. Megan's all right but I'm still not sure if her dad's told her to look out for me and anyway, I'm wary now of becoming close friends with someone. Close friends have a way of turning against you when the chips are down.

I'm never going to talk to any of my old friends again. I even threw my mobile in the canal so I wouldn't be tempted.

I wish I hadn't done that now.

It's too warm to sleep. I get out of bed and lift up the

old sash window, then I kneel on the floor and lean out, breathing deeply. It's pitch black outside and there are no streetlamps to pierce the night, just the lights of the occasional car on the distant road sweeping the tops of the hedges. I can vaguely make out the dark shapes of cows huddled together in the field on the other side of the lane. A dog barks in the distance then everything is quiet. An unearthly hush descends to lurk behind hedgerows, threatening and powerful.

I hate the silence of the countryside with a vengeance. I crave the noises of city life: car doors banging, people talking, bickering, laughing, cats yowling, police sirens wailing.

A twig snaps in the garden below. My eyes turn towards the sound and narrow as I peer into the darkness and I freeze.

Someone is standing by our garden gate.

I don't know if I imagined it but it really spooks me out, I can tell you. I pull back away from the window, cracking my head on the frame in the process, and yank the curtains together, then I stand up, my back against the wall, forcing myself to take deep breaths till I've calmed down. When my heart's stopped racing I peep through the curtains. The moon's come out now from behind the clouds and the garden is bathed in a silvery light. There's no one there.

Idiot. Of course there isn't. What was I expecting to find? A Peeping Tom here in the middle of nowhere? Or the ghost of some lost soul from the past come to study his old haunts? Hah! Old haunts, get it? It was probably one of those daft cows that had wandered over to sample the rhododendron bush in the front garden.

Do cows sleep or do they stand and chew grass all night long? Don't ask me.

I get into bed and curl myself round Izzy's warm body. She grumbles in her sleep and wriggles away. Before long I hear Mum stumbling up the stairs to her bedroom and soon the house is sleeping.

Life settles into a pattern. Bus to school. I sit with the smokers now though I won't join in. I don't have any choice really; Holly calls me up to the back every morning when I get on the bus and it would be churlish to refuse. Darren continues to annoy me but the others are all right, though I stink like an old ash tray by the time we get to school.

Jem sits in the middle. When he got on the bus the day after I waited for him, I thought he might come and explain why he stood me up. But when he saw me at the back with the others his lip curled in derision and that really cheesed me off, I can tell you.

'I can't stand cigarette smoke,' he'd said.

I was so mad I grabbed the cigarette from Holly's fingers and took a drag, eyeballing him as I blew the smoke out, just to show I didn't care. It put me off smoking for life, I can tell you. My eyes were watering as I struggled not to gag and cough at the same time, but it did the trick. He shook his head then slouched down in his seat, looking superior, and he's never so much as looked at me since.

I mean, who does he think he is? That's the last time I'll ever wait around for a bloke.

At school I hang around with Megan and Holly and all their mates. Mr Davey was right, people are friendly on the whole. I always keep a bit of me to myself though. No more outbursts like the one I had with Jem. I keep my head down and get on with my work, get my homework in on time, meet up with Megan and Holly on Saturdays and spend Sundays with Izzy and Mum. When Mr Davey meets me in the corridor he says, 'Everything all right, Kally?' and I smile and say, 'Yes, thank you, Mr Davey, everything's fine.'

But it's not. I'm bored out of my mind.

The thing is, there's nothing to doooooo.

I know that's the cry of every teenager, but in my case it's true, because now there's a huge gap in my life, like an aching great chasm. And for once I'm not talking about Dad not being around, though it's all tied up with him of course.

It's because I don't skate any more. Nobody seems to down here.

I don't mean ice-skating. I mean skateboarding.

You see I've spent the last couple of years skating and it's been a huge part of my life. In fact, if I hadn't been part of that scene, Dad would still be around and I'd still be at Deanswood with my old mates, and Mum would be lively and fun and have a life and Izzy . . . well, no, she'd probably still be performing frontal lobotomies on plastic dolls.

I got involved when I started secondary school and I had a skateboard for my birthday. There was a group of about five to ten of us, boys mostly and Ella and me, who used to hang out in the evenings and weekends, in playgrounds and car parks or just round town, trying to find new places and obstacles to pull tricks on. When it was wet we couldn't skate so we'd go back to my place and watch skate videos. That's how Dad got caught up in it.

'It looks brilliant that.' He'd come in from work to find us all glued to the television watching some guys performing tricks. 'Reckon I'm too old to start?'

'Yes, Dad,' I said, alarmed at the thought of my dad suddenly joining our set complete with baggy jeans, T-shirt and hoody. 'Way too old!'

'You'd break your neck!' laughed Mum. (She was always laughing in those days.)

But he was only teasing, thank goodness. Before long though, as I became more immersed in the scene, he got more interested. He was like that, my dad, always getting involved in what I was doing, not in a creepy I-don't-have-a-life-so-I'll-live-my-daughter's, pushy-parent way, but just by being supportive.

Like when I was at primary school he'd turn out on a Saturday morning to train the footy team. Not that I played football, but just because there was no one else willing to do it. He was on the PTA as well and always seemed to be devising great ways of raising money for the school, like Fantasy Fun Days where we all paid to dress up as our favourite fantasy character and do crazy things all day long, or Activity Days which involved lots of bouncy castles and silly races and dousing teachers with water. Everyone loved him, even the teachers who grumbled and groaned but always turned out to have wet sponges thrown at them, and especially the kids who wished he was their dad, and I was sooo proud of him.

So it was kind of inevitable that he got drawn into the skating scene. One Saturday I came home in a foul mood and flung myself on the sofa where Dad was watching the football on the telly.

'It's not fair!'

I remember it like yesterday. Dad goes, 'What's up, strop-face?' but he's not really listening. It's the last few minutes of the match, so I sit there fuming (I was really good at fuming when I was twelve) until the whistle blows and Dad yells, 'YES!' and punches the air with his hand. Then he says, 'Who's rattled your cage?'

'We've been chucked out of the church car park.'

'Not very Christian of the vicar. Why did he do that?' He takes a swig of tea out of a steaming mug Mum's just brought in.

'There was a wedding on.'

He chokes and tea spurts from his mouth like a fountain. Mum thumps his back and tells him off, then Izzy has to thump his back too and look in his mouth because even at that age, four or whatever, she's interested in the things that go wrong with bits of your body. By the time they've finished, tears are streaming down Dad's cheeks and everyone's laughing, including me.

'He's got a point, Kathryn. I mean, no bride wants a pack of skaters in hoodies zooming round her wedding photos!'

'Yeah, but now we've got nowhere to go!'

'What about school?'

'Locked up.'

'Superstore?'

'Told us to scram.'

'Industrial estate?'

'Told us to get lost.'

'Bus station?'

'Told us to b★★★★r off.'

Izzy seizes on this new extension to her vocabulary with delight, repeating it explosively which makes me and

Dad fall about laughing again but Mum tells us all off.

'You shouldn't be hanging round these places causing a nuisance to other people. It's dangerous for a start. You could get knocked over.'

'We've got no choice. We've got to skate somewhere. What do you suggest, the motorway?'

That's when Dad hits on his big idea.

'You need a skate-park.'

'Duh! Like we never thought of that!'

Crikey. What an obnoxious kid I was in those days. It's a wonder my dad bothered to speak to me, let alone went out of his way to help me. He seemed to think it was funny though.

'Right then, misery-guts. Project Skate Zone. We're going to get the council to build one!'

That was my dad.

Kids' champion.

Defender of the young.

Campaigner for children's rights.

Voice-piece for juveniles who no one else would listen to.

Citizen of the Year.

Liked and admired by adults, loved and respected by me and all my mates.

My father. My hero.

Sundays are rubbish.

'Family time', Mum calls it. Big joke.

Family time is going out for the day to an adventure park and screaming with terror and delight as your heart drops into your boots on the scary rides, but you know you're going to be OK because your dad is there keeping you safely anchored in his arms, while your mum looks on with her heart in her mouth and struggles to keep your little sister from joining you. Then it's filling up with fish and chips on the way home or even, best treat of all, a stop-off at your favourite fast-food chain.

'Ah, Jan, it's only once in a while!' Dad would say as Izzy and I gorged on the forbidden fruits of processed food while Mum angsted about our fat and salt intake. Those were the days.

Now Izzy has a better social life than I do. She's been invited to her friend Molly's birthday party and she's talked about nothing else all week.

Yesterday, she and Mum went to town and bought a card and a present for Molly (Operation, Izzy's favourite game) and when they came home Mum wrapped it up in shiny paper while Izzy, with her tongue clenched between her teeth in concentration, signed the card in her best round handwriting and drew stars and suns and stick friends labelled Izzy and Molly all over it. Then Mum made spag bog for us and opened a bottle of wine and poured herself a glass. We watched Saturday night telly together and it was almost like old times. Only Dad wasn't there to share the wine with Mum.

Nowadays days are divided into MUM'S GOOD DAYS and MUM'S BAD DAYS. She can't even be bothered to cook on a BAD DAY. Yesterday was a GOOD DAY.

But today Mum hasn't appeared yet.

So Izzy gets herself ready in a lurid pink net fairy costume she had for Christmas and a sparkly pyjama top she's been wearing to bed for a week and she's twirling around in excitement on plastic high heels that came with the costume and I haven't got the heart to tell her she looks feral. But then she gets giddy and falls off her heels on to me on the sofa, where I'm reading last month's magazine for the umpteenth time, and I snap, 'Go and tell Mum you're ready!' and Izzy stumbles off to find her fairy godmother to take her to the ball.

Only the fairy godmother's turned into the wicked witch. After a while Izzy reappears, her face pinched and crumpled.

'Mum's got one of her Me-grains,' she says dolefully. 'She says we can't go to the party.'

I look at her sad little face with all the joy and light drained out of it and I feel soooo angry with my mum. And if that makes me sound heartless then tough, I'm a freak, born without a heart, because these 'Me-grains' of Mum's are doing my head in. I know, they're doing hers in too, but it's pretty obvious to me that they come on conveniently when she can't face doing something. She never used to have them when Dad was at home.

I stamp upstairs to her bedroom. She's lying face down in bed in darkness with the curtains drawn. The room smells stuffy.

'Izzy's crying her eyes out downstairs.'

She lifts her head up to peer at me and groans.

'I'm sorry, Kally, I can't take her. My head's throbbing and I feel sick. Can you look after her?'

'And do what?'

'I don't know. Play with her or something. Take her for a walk.'

Izzy pushes past me into the room. 'I don't *want* to go for a walk! I want to go to the party!' She grabs hold of

Mum's hand and pumps it up and down in desperation. '*Please*, Mum.'

Mum buries her face in the pillows again. Her voice is muffled. 'I can't drive like this, Izzy. It wouldn't be safe.'

I stiffen. I've just noticed something by the side of the bed. It's last night's wine bottle and it's empty.

Migraine? I don't think so. Izzy's face is desolate. I hate Mum.

'Come on then, I'll take you.'

Izzy's face lights up. Mum protests, 'You can't, it's miles away, the other side of town.'

'So? We'll get the bus.'

'There isn't one on a Sunday.'

'We'll walk then! Come *on*, Izzy!' I grab my little sister by the hand and pull her downstairs before I change my mind. It's not fair. She snatches up the present and card and stumbles after me in her plastic heels as I stalk up the road. After a while I relent and wait for her to catch me up. She's put her foot through the net fairy skirt and there's a big hole in it and her hair's all over the place. She looks a mess.

'It's a long way to walk. Sure you want to go?'

She nods emphatically, her eyes round and trusting, chest heaving from the effort of trying to keep up with me. Poor Izzy. She doesn't complain like she used to, she knows there's no point. I think back to the parties Mum used to take me to at Izzy's age, dressed up like a freaking princess, and, with a sigh, kneel down to tuck her in properly, tying a knot in the elastic waist of the fairy skirt to keep it up. Then I smooth down her hair and stand up.

'Come on then.' We march along the road hand in hand so I can yank her back upright when she falls off her shoes, singing Izzy's favourite song together at the tops of our voices, the one that goes, 'Your kneebone's connected to your shin-bone'.

We stride past herds of solemn, chewing cows that moo appreciatively at our singing which makes Izzy giggle and stop to take a bow. We take short cuts through fields of sprouting green stuff, criss-crossed by footpaths and electricity pylons.

We pass clusters of cottages huddled together on the side of the road like village gossips and Izzy's primary school, an imposing remnant of the Victorian period, still with the signs 'BOYS' and 'GIRLS' etched sternly into the separate entrances. I give Izzy a quick leg-up as we go by to peer through a high window plastered with brightly-coloured-in butterflies. All is well. Her classroom is still there, waiting for her.

Then on we go through the empty streets of the town, shop doors closed in this remote granite corner where the council assumes people still keep the Sabbath, past the bus station and the locked gates of STC, playground eerily empty. On and on, till, at last, Izzy comes to a standstill in front of a detached house with a huge garden festooned with balloons where hundreds of little girls are charging round in their best frills and fancy, shrieking at the tops of their voices.

And I look at Izzy standing there, her face a picture of delighted anticipation under her messy hair, net skirt hanging down to her ankles, clutching her present and card, grubby now after being dropped once or twice on the way, and my heart sinks. I make a silent vow. If these kids give her a hard time I will personally kill them all.

'Go on!' I give her a gentle push but suddenly she's reluctant, as if my unease has seeped through to her, and I feel her pressing herself against me as her finger wraps round her nose and her thumb seeks the comfort of her mouth. And I'm exasperated now. I haven't legged it miles across country for nothing, and I'm about to tell her so in no uncertain terms when all at once an immaculate kid, hair neatly braided and dressed up to the nines, detaches herself from the shrieking, giggling profusion of little girls and squeals, 'Izzy!' She dashes towards her, seizing the present from her clutch, and tears the wrapping off. 'Operation!' she whoops, then the celebrated Molly Moulton enfolds my scruffy little sister in her arms like a long-lost friend.

There's a huge cheer and the others rush to swoop

on Izzy who's lost from sight inside a mass hug, and when she emerges, all pink and beaming from ear to ear, she spots me still standing there and says, 'Go *on*, Kally,' and turns on her plastic high heels to chase her fan club back up the garden. I don't know whether to be annoyed at being dismissed like an unwanted present or amused by her transformation from Shrinking Violet to Miss Popularity.

There's one thing for sure, I'm not needed here for the rest of the afternoon.

Which leaves me the next few hours to fill. I wander back towards the centre but all the shops are closed and there's no one around, just a couple of winos arguing beneath a 'No Alcohol' sign. I keep my head down as I pass them, not wanting any trouble, and turn the corner.

Then I spot him.

Baggy jeans, black hoody and, today, a beanie pulled down over his thick dark hair.

But still, unmistakably, Jem.

He's on his own, skating a set of steps outside the town hall. As I watch he does a massive kick-flip down the steps but doesn't quite land it and falls on his back.

I think that's the end because he looks in pain but he scrambles back up and tries again. This time he nails it, the board spinning perfectly beneath his feet, and he catches it cleanly just before he lands.

'That was huge.'

His head jerks up in surprise.

'How long have you been skating?' I ask.

'How long have you been watching me?'

'Not long.'

'Same here.'

'That's pretty technical for not long.'

He grins and bends down to pick up his board.

'Why are you so interested. Do you skate?'

'I've done a bit.'

He hands me the board. 'Wanna try?'

I consider, running my hands along the deck. It's been a long time and I vowed I would never pick up a skateboard again, but the temptation's too great. I skate about a bit to get the feel of the board and then I try a few simple tricks, the board staying nice and level as I soar in the air. Easy.

'You're a natural,' Jem says.

I nod in agreement. I know what he means. He's not saying I'm good, he's saying I skate with my right foot at the back.

'Like you. I recognized the shoe.' I glance down at his foot. When you're a natural skater, your left shoe takes all the scraping from the ground and gets worn through. It was practically the first thing I noticed about him.

'Takes one to know one. Can you do a shove-it?'

'Yeah.' I demonstrate the 180-degree turn of the board.

A bit rusty, but I manage it. This time he looks impressed.

'Kick-flips?'

'No way!'

'It's only practice. Want to try some tricks?'

We collect stuff that's strewn around, some rocks, a traffic cone, and take turns over it. He's good, really good, but he doesn't mind showing me what to do and soon I'm trying stuff I've never done before. It's ace. I'm concentrating so hard I don't notice how quickly the time's going. I can't remember when I enjoyed myself so much.

Then the clock on the town hall chimes six. I freeze, like Cinderella at the stroke of midnight.

'Flipping heck. I gotta go. I've got to pick up my sister.'

Jem comes to a halt and steps off the board. 'You're good,' he says. 'Come along tomorrow after school?'

I hesitate. He says quickly, 'Look, I'm sorry I didn't meet you the other night. I forgot I had a detention. With Whingy Walker.'

Of course. 'Why didn't you say?'

'I was going to,' he says, looking embarrassed. 'But you seemed to prefer sitting with the losers. You acted like you didn't want to know.'

He was right, I had. 'Sorry about that,' I say. 'Misunderstanding.'

'Shall we start again?'

I nod decisively. 'You bet.'

'See you here tomorrow then after school?'

'OK.'

His eyes crinkle.

'Good. It's a date.'

My heart beats fast and I can feel my colour rising and I run off quickly before he sees me blush, round the corner and through the shopping centre, ignoring the shouts of the two winos whose drunken reverie I disturb as I dash past.

At the end of the mall I slow down to get my breath and glance back. Jem appears on his skateboard, carving from side to side, and the alkies yell at him too and one struggles to his feet but Jem sweeps past and disappears round a corner leaving the guy shouting abuse after him. What is it about skaters that enrages the general public?

Mind you, Jem did make a very rude gesture.

By the time we get home, me dragging a now dead-weight Izzy, dog-tired with partying, back along the roads (I even carry her across the fields), the moon is up and I expect to see Mum on the doorstep beside herself with worry, but the house is in darkness and then *I'm* worried. Where can she be? I let us in with my key and switch the light on and call, 'Mum?' but there's no answer.

'Where is she?' Izzy's face is pinched with exhaustion.

'Popped in to see a neighbour,' I lie. 'Up to bed quick,

before she comes back and sees you're still up.'

Izzy scuttles upstairs and I go into the kitchen to find something to eat. I'm starving, unlike Izzy who's full of party tea. Our breakfast bowls from this morning are still in the sink. Where the hell is she? I pour myself a glass of milk then make myself a cheese sandwich and take it into the lounge to eat while I figure out what to do next.

The real truth is, I haven't got a clue where she could be. She doesn't know any of the neighbours down the lane, she keeps herself away from them on purpose. She actually doesn't know a soul in this neck of the woods; apart from doing some shopping and taking Izzy to and from school, she never goes out, just the occasional sneaky furtive foray to the phone box at the end of the lane. I know she goes there to talk to Dad.

Because that's another thing. We don't have a phone connected yet. I'm not sure we ever will have, given the precarious present state of our finances. Anyway, who would I phone?

We're all on own here. Mum, Izzy and me. And now Mum's disappeared. The house feels cold, dark and spooky. I hate it here.

I reach up for the throw draped over the back of the sofa and curl myself up inside it. There's nothing I can do but wait.

The next thing I know, the sun's up and Izzy's sitting cross-legged on the floor beside me, eating a bowl of cornflakes, still dressed in her fairy costume and pyjama top. She's slept in them. The contents of her party bag are arranged neatly around her bowl.

'Did you sleep here?' she asks. 'I'm telling Mum.' Milk drips from her spoon on to the rug. Her cornflakes are looking very colourful. She's emptied a box of Smarties into them.

I register what she's just said.

'Where is she?'

'Still in bed.' I sit up and rub my eyes. This is surreal. Did I dream she'd abandoned us last night? I look at my watch and jump up.

'MUM!' I yell up the stairs. 'Get a move on! It's late!'

There's a mumble from upstairs and soon Mum appears in her nightie, holding her head. I look at her suspiciously but it's obvious she's ill. Her eyes are streaming and she's clutching a sodden hanky to her nose. 'Can you take her, Kally? I feel terrible.'

'I can't! I'll be late for school!'

'I'll write you a note.' She breaks off in a spasm of coughing. 'Please, Kally?'

She sounds desperate.

'Where were you last night?'

'What do you mean?'

'We came home and you weren't here. The house was in darkness.'

'I was in bed! I stayed in bed all day, nursing this cold. I think it might be flu. I must have dropped off to sleep at last; I didn't hear you come in.'

'Kally said you were next door.' Izzy pops up, her face righteous. 'You told a lie, Kally.'

Mum's face softens. 'Thanks for that.'

'Just let me know where you are next time!'

I'm like an angry mother telling her teenage daughter off for staying out late, then Mum says quietly, 'Oh Kally love, you didn't think I'd deserted you, did you? I'd never do that,' and I'm about six again and all I want is to fling myself into her arms and feel them tight around me, keeping me safe.

You see, last night I was scared stiff I'd lost my mum as well. And then I don't know what I'd do.

‘Go back to bed then,’ I say gruffly. ‘I’ll get Izzy ready.’ She smiles gratefully and turns and shuffles back upstairs.

‘Clean your teeth,’ I say to Izzy and go to search for her school uniform. It’s not there.

‘It’s in the wash,’ says Izzy, hopping round in her vest and pants, spattering toothpaste everywhere. At least she’s taken her pyjama top off for the first time in days. Gritting my teeth, I rummage through the laundry basket, pulling out the least grubby polo top and skirt I can find. I sniff them cautiously. Dab them with water, run the iron over them and they’d have to do.

I put my head round Mum’s door. She’s back in bed, propped up against the pillows. ‘We’re off now. Izzy’s got no clean clothes left for school.’

‘I’ll see to it. Thanks, Kally.’

‘You need to go to the doctor’s,’ I say.

She sniffs. ‘I think I will. Would you pick her up after school for me?’

Jem! I go to protest but she looks terrible so I nod and she says, ‘Thanks, Kally,’ and sinks down gratefully into the bed, pulling her duvet round her. It’s not till we’re halfway along the road that I realize I’ve forgotten the note.

By the time I’ve dropped Izzy off and waited for the next bus, I’m seriously late. I sign my name in the late book and set off to find my class who are halfway through the first lesson. It's Technology and they're all split up into different groups and I don't know where I'm supposed to be. I wander along the corridors, peering into classrooms, hoping to find a face I recognize.

I do. Whingy Walker's. Trust. She's writing on the whiteboard in front of a class that are visibly yawning and bored to tears. It's Year 10, I can see Jem at the back. He smiles and raises a hand. I walk on quickly but it's too late, she's spotted me.

'Kally O'Connor?' I turn to face her as she comes out in the corridor and glares at me, hands on her hips. 'Come here!'

I retrace my footsteps slowly. She moves back into the classroom. I remain outside. 'Come in, come in. I've got a class to teach, you know.'

So get on with it and leave me alone! Reluctantly I enter the room, keeping my eyes glued to the floor, but I can sense the class perking up instantaneously. My heart sinks.

'What are you doing wandering round the corridors?'

'Trying to find my lesson, Miss.'

'Trying to find my lesson, *Mrs* Walker.' She studies me with dislike. The feeling is reciprocal. I wait for her to tell me where it is. Too logical.

'Why are you late for school?'

I can feel the whole class waiting for my answer. It's

got to be more entertaining than Walker's tortuous dissection of 'The Ancient Mariner'.

'I had to take my sister to school.'

'Where is your note?'

'I forgot it.'

Someone near the front tuts ironically. There's a ripple of laughter. Mrs Walker bristles.

'Why didn't your mother take her?'

'She's not well.'

'What's wrong with her?'

For goodness' sake! Bipolar disorder. Multiple sclerosis. Cancer. What do you want me to say? Mind your own business, you old bag.

'She's got the flu.'

'She's got the flu!' She repeats this as if it's the most ridiculous thing she's ever heard. I can hear the class tittering. I don't know if they're laughing at her getting in a tizz or me looking stupid. My cheeks flame.

'And what about your father? Why couldn't he take your sister to school?'

I stand there paralysed, face on fire, body icy cold.

'I'm waiting.'

You can wait as long as you like, you evil cow, this is the one question I can't answer.

The silence extends as the whole class waits to find out where my father is.

'Look at me when I'm talking to you. I asked you a question.'

I raise my eyes, which have been riveted to a stain on the floor, to meet hers; her irises are a washed-out blue and the whites are threaded with tiny red veins. They're bulging with anticipation and her eyebrows are raised ludicrously above them, creasing her forehead into wavy lines. Close up, her skin is mottled with sunspots.

There is nothing I can say.

'Dumb insolence!' A tiny ball of spittle spurts from her mouth and clings to her lips which are pursed with venom. 'Go to Mr Davey's office and tell him I've sent you for being impertinent.'

I gasp with the injustice of it all and turn to make my escape.

'That's not fair. She hasn't done anything.'

The voice comes from the back of the class. Jem is leaning back on his chair, rocking it gently on its two back legs, a pen in his mouth.

'How dare you!' spits Walker. 'Sit up properly!'

Jem lets the front legs of his chair fall forward with a bang. He takes the pen from his mouth and spreads his hands wide to appeal to his audience. 'Did she do anything? I didn't see her. Did you?'

People start laughing. 'I never!'

'Not me!'

'She didn't do nothing!'

'It's not fair!'

The classroom buzzes with denials as people seize the opportunity for disruption. Mrs Walker looks alarmed.

'THAT'S ENOUGH!'

Silence falls momentarily but Jem presses home his advantage.

'You shouldn't ask questions like that. It's not right. Her father could be dead for all you know.'

'Yeah, dead and buried.'

'Six foot under.'

'Or cremated! My granddad was cremated.'

'Your granddad was an idiot!'

'No he wasn't! You are!'

'You are!'

A ball of screwed-up paper follows this remark and finds its target. Mayhem breaks out. Jem smiles at me and winks as people exploit the situation for all it's worth. I cast a quick glance at Mrs Walker who looks as if she's going to have a blue fit (and now I know what they mean by that expression because the skin around her mouth, all puckered up into a tight, furious rose, has taken on a curious blue tinge), then all of a sudden, silence falls and everyone bows their heads to study their poetry books with intense interest.

'Would anyone like to tell me what is going on?'

Mr Davey is standing in the doorway. He frowns at me. 'Kally? What are you doing in here?'

'I'm trying to find my lesson, Sir.'

'Year 9? They've got Technology now. You're down to do Food in the Technology Centre if I remember rightly.'

Why couldn't the Dag have just told me that and saved all this hassle? I go to move past him but she screeches, 'Not so fast! You're going nowhere, young lady, disrupting my lesson like that. I was just about to send her to see you, Mr Davey, for being impertinent. And Jermaine Smith as well!'

Strange that. The class have suddenly become more interested in the plight of 'The Ancient Mariner' than in defending my innocence. All except Jem who's watching the proceedings with an expression of faint amusement on his face.

Not Mr Davey's favourite expression if I remember rightly. 'Report to me at breaktime, both of you,' he says, tight-lipped. 'Now, Kally, off to your lesson. And the rest of you, get on with your work!'

I slip into Food Technology quietly. The teacher, round and middle-aged and in the middle of a demonstration, raises her eyebrows and asks, 'Problem?' and I nod and she says, 'Just watch carefully, you haven't missed much,' and I raise a silent prayer that there are some sensible teachers at STC and settle down to learn how to make a vegetarian supper. Then we write down the ingredients to bring for next week and sample the dish when she takes it out of the oven. Delicious.

At breaktime I make my way to Mr Davey's office and perch on one of the 'naughty' chairs outside. I suppose this is progress of sorts: this time last month I was just the NEW GIRL; now I'm an official BAD GIRL. I haven't done anything wrong so I don't care, except I'm worried I'll be banged up in detention and then I won't be able to pick Izzy up from school.

Jem comes slouching along, hands in his pockets. He grins when he sees me and says, 'All right?'

I nod. 'Thanks for sticking up for me.'

'My pleasure.' He gives me a mock bow. 'We're quits now.' The door opens and Mr Davey barks, 'Come in, both of you,' and Jem follows me inside, stuffing his shirt inside his trousers. I don't know why schools just don't declare shirts hanging out of skirts and trousers as regular school uniform. It would save teachers repeating, 'Tuck your shirt in,' three hundred times a day. But then they'd find something else to stress about. Mr Davey points to two seats and sits down opposite.

'Now then, what was all that about?'

Jem outlines what happened quickly and simply.

'Mrs Walker made Kally come into our classroom and

asked her personal questions about her family in front of us all.'

'Is this true, Kally?'

I nod.

'Did you answer Mrs Walker back?'

'No, Sir.'

'And what was your role in this, Jem?'

'He stuck up for me, Sir.'

'Hmm. Rudeness to teachers cannot be tolerated.' He picks up a pile of yellow detention slips from the desk. My heart takes a dive.

'Don't put us in detention, not tonight. I've got to pick up my little sister from school. Please, Sir . . .'

'I couldn't detain you tonight if I wanted to. We give at least twenty-four hours' notice here for detention.' He studies me carefully then taps the slips into a neat pile and puts them into his top drawer. 'Anyway, I think in this case an apology from you will suffice. You will go and see Mrs Walker at the end of the day and tell her you are sorry for disrupting her lesson. Both of you.'

I swallow. What have I got to apologize for? I open my mouth to protest but Mr Davey shakes his head. 'Don't even think about it, Kally. You've got off lightly, believe me.' He stares at Jem. 'And so have you.'

Jem shrugs.

'Now scoot before I change my mind.' He holds the

door open for us. Jem goes out first and as I go to pass Mr Davey, I glance up and say, 'Thanks, Sir.' I'm not stupid, I can tell he's gone out on a bit of a limb for me.

'Stay away from him,' he says quietly, nodding towards Jem's back, then he closes the door. It was so quick I wonder if I imagined it.

Outside, Jem grins at me. 'Nice one. Liked the bit about having to pick up your little sister.'

'It's true.'

His grin fades.

'I thought we were going to do some skating?'

'I'm sorry, I can't. My mum's ill.'

His eyes narrow. I'm not sure if he believes me or not. Then he says, 'Tell you what, I'll come with you to collect your sister, OK?'

I stare at him in surprise. 'Yeah. That'll be cool.' A thought occurs to me. 'After we've been to apologize to the Dag.'

'The Dag. I like it. Nice one, Kally.' His face, normally dark and brooding, lights up and for the first time that day I feel as if the sun's come out from behind my own personal cumulus nimbus that seems to permanently hang over me, and I bask in the warmth of his smile.

The Dag keeps us waiting. On purpose. Her class are late out anyway because she's telling them off and then, when she spots us, she prats about pretending to tidy up before finally beckoning us in.

'Yes?' she barks.

'Mr Davey sent us here to apologize, Miss.'

'Mr Davey sent us here to apologize, *Mrs Walker*.'

She lives her life like Groundhog Day, every sentence repeated once, no twice, by the time we intone it back to her, just so she can hear her rightful married title. I wonder what poor Mr Walker is like and if he has to repeat everything too and stifle an overwhelming desire to giggle as my imagination runs riot.

She spouts on about RUDENESS and COURTESY and RESPECT and THE PROPER WAY TO BEHAVE, her thought processes a loop that goes on and on like schmaltzy music in a department store.

At last she runs out of steam and, assuming we are suitably repentant (wrong!), lets us go. I'm now seriously late to pick up Izzy.

Jem's got his board with him so we take it in turns to skate along the road on it while the other one legs it behind. When we get to the school there are no kids or mums hanging about; the playground's empty and the main door is closed. My heart sinks.

'Where is she? Where's Izzy?'

I spot a light on in her classroom. Jem gives me a leg-up and I peer through the high window. Izzy is bowed over a table sticking paper on to card, deep in concentration. Behind her, a young teacher, slim and blonde, is pinning things to the wall.

'She's there!' I rap on the window. Both faces look up and Izzy beams and waves then turns back to her gluing. Her teacher points to the GIRLS entrance.

'This way!' I push open the door and we run down the corridor round to Izzy's classroom. All the rest of the rooms are in darkness, there's no one else left in the school. I burst into the classroom. 'I'm *so* sorry!' This time I mean it. 'I got kept behind at school, there was nothing I could do!'

'That's OK. We've been busy, haven't we, Izzy? She's been helping me put up a display.'

'We haven't finished yet,' said Izzy, wielding her

glue stick officiously. 'You can come back later if you want.'

'Actually, I think that will do nicely for today, Izzy. You've been a great help,' the teacher says hastily, smiling at me and Jem. 'You must be Kally. I've heard all about you.'

'Have you?' I look at Izzy suspiciously. What else has she said?

'I'm Miss Baker by the way.' She shakes hands with me then extends hers to Jem. 'And who are you?'

Jem eyes her appreciatively. No wonder, she's gorgeous. She's got blonde spiky hair and big brown eyes with sweeping eyelashes and she's stick-thin. I should hate her but she's got a lovely big smile (with perfect white teeth, of course) and she's nice to my weird little sister so I don't.

'I'm Jem. A friend of Kally's.'

'No you're not.' Izzy peers at Jem suspiciously. 'Kally hasn't got any friends.'

Miss Baker giggles with embarrassment, sounding more like someone my age than a teacher. 'Oh, I'm sure that's not true, Izzy.'

'It is,' says Izzy matter-of-factly. 'Not any more.'

'She has now,' says Jem. 'Come on, I'm going to walk you home.'

I feel warmth coursing through my veins and I

turn to Miss Baker as we go. 'Sorry again for being late.'

'Don't worry about it; I'm always here till late. Look,' she scribbles on a piece of paper and hands it to me, 'take my mobile number and if it happens again, just give me a ring. The office staff disappear as soon as the bell goes.'

'She's nice, isn't she?' I say to Jem as we exit the school.

He nods appreciatively. 'I'd swap her for the Dag any day!'

We set off along the road together. Jem asks Izzy all about school and friends and teachers and my little sister chats away nineteen to the dozen, revelling in the attention. She seems to know everything there is to know about Miss Baker, whose first name is Laura, who has just finished with her boyfriend, rents a flat in town and likes to eat pizza. What is it with little kids and their teachers? The less I know about them, the better. It gets boring after a while but Jem makes a good job of feigning interest.

When she's exhausted her fund of information Jem tells her some really corny jokes that have her falling about in fits of giggles then, when she gets tired, he gives her a piggyback on his skateboard which she thinks is amazing. By the time we get home, she is totally besotted.

'Here you are,' he says, turning into our lane and

depositing her at the gate to our cottage. 'One parcel safely delivered.'

'How did you know this was my house?' I ask in surprise. For a moment he looks disconcerted. Then he shrugs. 'I didn't. I just guessed.'

Guessed? Out of all the little granite cottages in this neck of the woods, he happened to pick the right one. Intuitive or what? I gaze up at the roof with clumps of grass growing out of the guttering and the window frames that need a lick of paint. It looks as if it needs some tender, loving care. Like me.

'Thanks,' I say as Izzy scampers into the house.

'What for?'

'Everything.'

'My pleasure.' Jem's eyes crinkle when he smiles. 'She's ace, your little sister. So, shall we try again sometime? Skating, I mean.'

'When Mum's better, yeah.' A warm feeling courses through me, one I haven't felt for a long time and it takes me a moment to recognize it. It's happiness.

'You don't happen to have a board of your own, do you?'

I take a deep breath, 'Actually, I do.'

'Sweet. Bring it with you when you're ready.'

I stand and watch as he goes off up the lane, returning his wave before he disappears round the corner. What I haven't told him is I'd put it away . . . and vowed never to use it again. My skating days were over for good as far as I was concerned.

But that was then, not now.

We'd worked our socks off, raising money for that skate-park. We emptied our cupboards and attics of all the paraphernalia left over from childhood and held garage sales, then put all the leftovers together and did a massive car-boot one Sunday morning, with the help of our dads. The mums baked cakes and we sold them at school and then they got together and held coffee mornings and cheese and wine evenings and bring-and-buy sales in each other's gardens.

Then my dad organized a pub quiz which was a great success, so my best friend Ella's dad held an auction of promises for us in his local, where people bid for things like an evening's babysitting or to have their car cleaned for a tenner. And then it just escalated; it was mind-blowing.

Soon there were events going on all over our neighbourhood: men were having their heads and legs shaved; women were bungee-jumping off the river bridge and abseiling from the church tower; kids were doing sponsored swims, runs and skates. Even the babies at the local crèche had a sponsored sleep-in.

It was a brilliant time because, apart from getting closer and closer to our goal, it was a real bonding exercise. Our school got behind us and we put on regular discos and all the mums and dads in the area got to mix with each other; there was always somebody or other having a barbecue or a garden party or a fun event of some kind for the skate-park. It kind of broke down the barriers and people got to know each other. Like Mum said, there was loads of goodwill directed towards us.

We got to be really famous; the local paper ran photos and articles about our fund-raising activities every week and Dad and I were interviewed on the radio. We became minor celebrities because it had all come from us, you see. And it wasn't long before we were on the telly, featured on the regional news, and after that, the money poured in, not just from the general public but from various grants and things that people had pointed out we were entitled to.

People like Emma Preston. She'd arrived one day in a smart suit and high heels, her long fair hair pinned up on top of her head escaping attractively from its jewelled clips, carrying a huge briefcase full of information.

'Who's she?' whispered Dad when he came home from work one day to find her ensconced on the sofa in our front room, chatting animatedly to Mum and sipping tea from one of our best cups. She was that type of person, Emma. She sort of demanded the best of everything without actually asking for it, if you know what I mean, as if it were her right.

'She told Mum she worked for one of those agencies set up to award funding to urban projects. She wants to help us.'

'I think I could be of use to you in securing and co-ordinating funding for this project of yours, Mr O'Connor,' she said, sitting there in her trendy grey suit with a glimpse of a white top, long legs crossed neatly at the knee. 'I could take some of the administrative weight off your shoulders, all the mundane things like planning and grants and tenders and health and safety and suchlike, leaving you free to get on with what you're good at, which is raising money with the general public.'

'Steve, please,' he said, staring at Emma as if she'd been wafted here from paradise. 'You reckon you could do all that?'

'Oh, I always get what I want, Steve.' She'd smiled at him, red lips parted to reveal pretty white teeth, exuding confidence. 'Just let me run through a few things with you and you'll see what I mean.'

Well, by the time she'd finished, Dad was hooked. She really knew her stuff, making short work of all the boring admin stuff Dad hated and, before long, he'd handed all that over to her to concentrate on being the front man.

Soon they were working together closely to set up the skate-park and, with Emma's help, the money continued to flood in, big-time.

Mum had got a bit fed up with the amount of time they were spending together but, like Dad said, we needed Emma, he was no good at that sort of thing. He was more the Face of the Skate-Park, the kind of person who could inspire others, bring the best out of them, so to speak.

'OUR LOCAL HERO' they called him in the paper. 'OUR MAN OF THE PEOPLE'. They were going to name the skate-park after him. The 'STEVE O'CONNOR SKATE-BOWL'. I was so proud of him.

And before long, we were ready to go. We'd raised a quarter of a million pounds through a mixture of private and government grants and public donation. We were soooo excited, our dream was about to come true at last.

Then the money disappeared.

At the weekend I get my skateboard down from the loft and dust it off. I run my hands over the distinctive board with its skull and crossbones, enjoying the contrast between the rough deck and the worn smoothness beneath, and spin the wheels and know I'm back with a long-lost friend. I can't wait to have a go, but the lane outside is unmade and the main road it branches off from is narrow and bending and far too dangerous.

On Monday morning, Mum's eyes open wide and her eyebrows shoot up to her hairline when she sees it by the front door waiting for me. I was wondering how she'd react.

'I've found someone who skates,' I say by way of explanation.

'Who?'

'Jem.'

'Jem, Jem, Jemmy, Jem, Jem,' sings Izzy. 'I love Jem.'

'The boy who walked you home the other day?'

I nod. 'He's in Year 10.'

'Jem, Jemmy, Jem, Jem,' Izzy carries on tunelessly. 'Kally loves Jem.'

'No I don't,' I say automatically. 'Shut up, nuisance.'

'It's nice to see you making friends.' I glance at Mum. She's on the mend now and looking more like her old self. Not her old, old self, the proper, functioning, happy pre-trouble Mum, just the old self before the bout of flu. She buttons Izzy into her school uniform and I notice how thin her wrists are.

'I might be late home. We're going skating after school.'

'Where?'

'I dunno. We'll have to find somewhere out of people's way. They could do with a skate-park here.' I could have bitten my tongue off as soon as I'd said it.

A bitter ghost of a smile hovers on Mum's lips as she finishes stuffing bits of Izzy into place and stands up. 'Sounds familiar. A touch of *déjà vu*.'

'What's "Day Sha Voo"?' asks Izzy.

'Something you've done before,' Mum explains. 'A blast from the past. Be careful, Kally.'

What does she mean? Don't fall off your skateboard? Unlikely. Don't skate because it leads to trouble? Possibly. Or don't blab to my new-found friend all about what happened before. Probably.

I feel a sudden surge of anger. I've done nothing wrong! Stop making me feel as if I've got something to hide.

When all the trouble had started Mum coped at first, convinced that it was all a big misunderstanding that would soon be sorted out. I don't know exactly what happened, but I remember it was around the time the construction of the skate-bowl was about to start. The company in charge had already cleared the ground and were ready to dig the foundations. Dad had written them a cheque as a deposit and we were all so excited about it when he sent it off, because at last it was all about to happen.

Anyway, this particular day, two policemen came to the door, asking to speak to Mr Stephen O'Connor, and Mum told me to go upstairs and play with Izzy while she and Dad went into the front room with them and shut the door. After a while Dad came out and got in the police car with them and drove away and Izzy bawled her head off because he hadn't said goodbye to us, but Mum said, 'Never mind, he'll be home soon, he's just helping them with their enquiries.'

'What enquiries?'

'Something to do with the skate-park. The money's disappeared,' said Mum, looking white-faced and worried. 'I'd better phone Emma, she'll sort it all out.'

Well, Emma tried, she went straight down the police station and stayed there all night answering questions and trying to work out where all the money had gone, but when Dad came home in the morning he said it was no good, it had vanished into thin air. He was so upset, he made loads of phone calls and after each one he got more bewildered and angry and he and Mum kept having urgent whispered conversations, in between telling me that everything was going to be fine.

But it wasn't, of course. Next day it was the talk of school because word had got around that the work on the skate-bowl had stopped before it had even started as someone had run off with the money. Everyone was asking me questions and I told them everything I knew, enjoying being the centre of attention. Soon the local paper got hold of the story and printed big banner headlines saying things like, 'WHO'S GOT OUR MONEY?' and 'OUR CHILDREN ROBBED!' with a picture of my skateboarding mates sitting on the kerb looking really miserable, but Mum wouldn't let me be in the photo because she said it was fuelling speculation, whatever that meant, and people had wicked minds.

Now that surprised me because Mum was always saying how good people were, especially when we were fund-raising, but then, one day, we were all walking down the street together and Ella's dad, who had organized the pub auction, was coming towards us and I went to say hello but suddenly he spat on the ground at my dad's feet and called him a filthy, horrible name. Dad went to hit him and I can't say I blamed him, I'd hit someone who called me that too, but Mum pulled him away.

It was only then I realized they were blaming my dad for stealing the money. And not long after that he was arrested and formally charged.

All those people who had helped us to raise the money turned against us. Most weren't as nasty as Ella's dad, they didn't swear at us in the street, but they avoided us as if we had the plague. It was as if we had a big black cross on our front door, no one came near us, and in the High Street people would cross the street if they saw us coming and shops would fall silent if we went in.

In school I tried to talk to Ella but she said she wasn't allowed to and went off with the others. I got into fights in the playground because kids would say nasty things about my dad and then I got into fights in the classroom and, in the end, it was decided I'd be better off at home till the trial was over.

The funny thing was, Mum held it together then. Through all that, she was the one who kept us all going. She would sail down the road with Izzy in tow, her head held high, saying 'Good morning!' or 'Good afternoon!' and daring people to ignore her. But Dad stayed at home, unable to face anyone, even though he'd been released on bail. He felt responsible for the money disappearing, you see, even though it was nothing to do with him.

'Don't you worry, Steve,' I remember Mum saying one day while he sat with his head in his hands. 'The truth will come out at this flaming trial and then they'll all be sorry!' She was brilliant, defiant and strong.

It was after the court case she went to pieces, when they sent my dad to prison.

Mum's right. It's better if I don't say anything about it at my new school. I keep my distance because, paradoxically, I don't want to be ostracized again. Not now I'm settling in at last.

It helps that I've started hanging out with Jem because he's a loner too. No one knows much about him, he keeps himself to himself, so people don't intrude on his space. Lots of the girls would like to get to know him better though. Holly, for instance. She can't believe I'm going skating with him after school. She stands there arm in arm with Megan, her eyes gawping.

'Lucky thing!' she breathes. 'You've got a date with Jem!'

'It's not a date!'

'He asked you to go skating with him. That's a date in my book.' She nudges Megan in the ribs. 'Here comes Lover Boy.' She watches as Jem approaches, his deck under his arm, then she says at the top of her voice, 'You know, I wouldn't mind learning to skate. Mind if I come along, Jem?'

I gasp. She's so pushy! OK, it's not a date, but she's still got a bare-faced cheek muscling in. And she's going to be a pain because she's never been on a skateboard in her life. I've been really looking forward to this. But I can't tell her she's not wanted, can I?

Jem doesn't share my reservations.

'Sorry. You're too heavy for a skateboard. When you've lost a bit of weight, maybe. Ready, Kally?'

He skates off. I take one look at Holly's furious face and jump on my board and chase after him, trying not to laugh. King of the put-down or what? Behind me I can hear Holly squeaking, 'Bloody cheek! I'm not fat! I knew it was a date.'

We have a brilliant time. We go down to the town hall again and practise some tricks. There are quite a few people around at first, on the way home from work, most of whom glare at us as if we're committing some crime, even though we're both experienced enough skaters to keep out of their way. It drives me mad the way some adults catch sight of a hoody and a skateboard and assume you're up to no good.

Soon the space in front of the hall empties out and we can try more complicated stuff. Jem is ace at street skating, grinding along a ledge and dropping down on to the pavement. He demonstrates his kick-flip, somersaulting his board and landing back on it safely. I try to copy him, again and again, but it's harder than it looks and I fall off and land on my back.

'Don't give up,' says Jem, hauling me to my feet. 'It's only practice.' His hands remains grasped round mine and he smiles and pulls me to him. His eyes grow serious as he looks down at me and everything goes still and I think, oh my goodness, he's going to kiss me! Then suddenly some bald bloke in a tight suit appears and barks, 'You two keep away from my car!' and points to a big, flashy saloon parked about a mile away and then he mutters, 'Bloody vandals,' and goes back into his office nearby. I glance at Jem and his face is tight and set.

The moment's gone. It's getting late and I've got to go, Mum will be worrying. Just as we're leaving, Jem suddenly says, 'Wait a minute,' and disappears behind the bald guy's car. There's a hissing noise.

'What are you doing?' I gasp. Jem stands up and grins. 'Just giving him what he asked for,' he says conversationally and gets on his board. I go to the other side of the car and gaze at the flat tyre. Automatically I look up at the office building and see the bald guy standing up and peering out of the window. Quickly I jump on my board and follow Jem, who's wending his way through the precinct.

And it occurs to me in bed that night that it might not be a good idea to get on the wrong side of Jem.

Jem's teaching me new tricks. I'm coming on under his guidance. I can't quite master a kick-flip yet, where the board spins in the air parallel to the ground before you land back on it, but I'm getting there.

'It's just practice,' he says and we're getting plenty of that. We go out after school when we can though we're careful not to keep going to the same place because people get fed up and tell you to clear off. It's better on a Sunday, you don't get so much hassle from the public.

The next time we go to the town hall the bald bloke comes out and yells at Jem. 'Hey, you! I want a word with you!'

Jem skates over to him casually, coming to a wide sweeping halt in front of him.

'Did you let down the tyre on my car?'

'Now why would I want to do a thing like that?'

The guy peers at him suspiciously, his eyes narrowed. He knows he's lying.

Actually, he's not. Jem's too clever for that. He's just not admitting the truth.

'Keep away from it,' he growls. Jem says nothing but gives him that smirk he's so good at, the one that infuriates everyone, where he barely lifts the corner of his mouth but manages to convey complete contempt. The guy looks as if he wants to smack him in it but resists and marches back to his office. Wise move.

You see, Jem can be two completely different people. It's like he's split down the middle, fifty/fifty, into Good Jem/Bad Jem. You don't want to mess with Bad Jem.

He can put people down so easily, with just a few well-chosen words. Like he did with Holly. Or if they're seriously annoying him, he has ways of dealing with that too. Like the bald guy. And like he did with Darren.

Let me explain.

There's been a flurry of interest in skateboarding since we've been bringing our boards to school. We're not allowed to use them in the yard of course, but a few people started tagging along with us after school, though no one was up to Jem's level or even mine come to that. I think Jem was quite flattered at first but soon it began to get on his nerves, probably because people kept asking him for advice. It's weird because he's patience personified with me, always encouraging me to aim a bit higher, take risks and all that, but he can't be bothered with anyone else.

Then one day, when we're skating in the park, Darren turns up, Piggy Darren from my class, in his stone-washed baggy jeans and a brand-new state-of-the-art board you'd die for. Ironic or what? I remember him saying, 'Boring,' when I read out my piece about skateboarding in class.

'Got it for my birthday,' he says, lording it a bit. 'My dad had it custom-made for me. It cost nearly two hundred quid counting the trucks, wheels and bearings.'

I could see Jem's lip curling before Darren had even got on it.

He wasn't bad actually, to be fair. He could do ollys, simple jumps that is, and a few other basic manoeuvres. Jem wasn't impressed though.

'All the gear, no idea,' he sneers.

'Give him a chance,' I say expansively, even though I'm no fan of Darren's. 'He's got to learn.'

I'm busy doing my own thing, trying to practise my pathetic attempts at the kick-flip, when I notice Jem is giving Darren some advice about a move. That's nice of him, I think, and stand and watch as Darren jumps off the board so Jem can use it to demonstrate a board slide. He builds up speed then ollys up on to the park bench, the middle of the board balanced on the edge. At the end of the move his feet part company with the board then he lands back heavily on it, splat in the middle, just as it hits the ground.

There's an ominous crack as the board splits in two. Jem falls forward, his arms splayed out before him, and lies still for a moment before he rolls over and sits up to examine his hands. The palms are torn to shreds and he tucks them under his armpits and groans. Everyone gathers round to see if he's OK except for Darren who silently picks up his deck now snapped into two pieces.

'Sorry, mate,' says Jem, his face screwed up with pain. 'I guess I've killed your board.'

Darren shrugs. 'Can't be helped,' he says, like he didn't care. 'As long as you're all right.' But I see his face as he turns away and he's gutted.

'How are your hands?' I ask Jem later on, as we say goodbye. He still hasn't kissed me yet but at least we're into hugs now. I guess it's just a matter of time.

'Stings a bit.' Jem studies his skinned palms then his face breaks into a grin. 'Worth it though, to see his face.'

I've seen Jem do that move a hundred times. He never puts a foot wrong.

See what I mean? You wouldn't want to upset him.

But then there's Good Jem. Who's kind to my little sister and will go out of his way to do anything for me.

Like the other day it's Megan's birthday and everyone's going down the juice bar in town for a celebratory drink after school, but I can't go because Mum's asked me to pick up Izzy from school.

'I'll get her if you like,' says Jem when I'm moaning to him at lunchtime. I stare at him in surprise.

'Would you?'

'Yeah, no problem. I'll drop her off at your house then you can take your time with Megan. Will your mum be there?'

I nodded. 'She's got some appointment but she'll be back by the time you've walked Izzy home. Tell you what,' a thought occurred to me, 'you'd better phone the school, tell them you'll be collecting Izzy. You know what they're like. Or better still, I've got Miss Baker's mobile number here. She said we could call her anytime. Sure you don't mind?'

''Course not. We're bezzies, Izzy and me.' He punches the number into his phone.

See what I mean? How many boys would do that for you, saddle themselves with your annoying little sister? Izzy was going to be made up.

When I get home that night, she's full of how Jem came to pick her up from school, how Jem chatted to Miss Baker, how Jem gave her a go on his skateboard (Izzy, not Miss Baker), how Jem bought her an ice-cream and let her choose the double chocolate and strawberry special, not the cheap orange lolly I always make her have, how Jem told her funny stories and how Jem was generally a laugh a minute all the way home.

'He's much more fun than you, Kally,' she points out unnecessarily. Then, 'I wish Jem could bring me home every day.' She goes on all night, Jem this, Jem that, till it does my head in. Then Mum starts.

'He seems a very nice boy, this Jem,' she says as soon as Izzy's finally in bed, having first lined up every one of her dolls and stuffed animals, all in various stages of life-threatening disease, in bed beside her, ready for a ward visit from Dr Jem, the new registrar, in the morning. I wish! There's a pause. I wait for the inevitable and manage to count twenty seconds before she says predictably, 'Are you going out with him, Kally?'

'Sort of.'

Another pause. Ten seconds this time. 'Be careful, won't you?'

'Of course I will,' I say, hoping she'll shut up.

'Because the less known about us the better, Kally. People can be very cruel.'

Not that again. Is that all she cares about? I know! I was the one who had fights in the playground, remember? I was the one who was forced out of school.

'You know, we've got to move on, Mum.' There's

silence. I've overstepped the mark. I turn to look at her. She's gnawing the side of her thumbnail, like she always does when she's worrying about something. Nowadays they look permanently raw. All of a sudden she bites decisively, removes the offending iota of skin from her tongue and sits up straight.

'You're right. I've got a job.'

'Have you?' I stare at her in disbelief. 'Where?'

'In the little general store next to the garage along the road. I've been there this afternoon for an interview. I'm just doing Mondays and Tuesdays, starting next week. You're going to have to pick up Izzy from school.'

'What?' I was planning to start netball training next week. Megan had taken me along to try out for the team. I'd been looking forward to it. Then I see Mum sitting there waiting for my response, and for the first time since we moved here I can see a sparkle, a hint of the old Mum. Her back is straight, her shoulders have lost that old-woman hunch, her eyes are bright and looking at me directly.

'I need to do something, Kal,' she says, 'before I go completely mad. Will you help?'

'You bet I will.' I get up and give her a hug. 'No problem.'

But there is of course. It means I don't get to train for netball and so I don't get to play in the team.

'It's not fair,' I whinge to Jem on Sunday. We're skating the town hall steps again. Jem does a brilliant grind down the handrail and leaps into the air. Me, I'm negotiating the kerb but my heart's not in it. In the end I sit on the ground and complain bitterly to Jem as he skates around me. 'I've been dying to get back into netball. But the two afternoons I have to pick up Izzy are the two afternoons they train.'

'That's all right, misery-guts,' he says, tugging my ponytail as he circles me. 'I'll do it for you.'

My head twists round to follow him. 'D'you mean it?'

'Yep.'

'What? Every week?' I scramble to my feet.

'Yep.'

'Jem!' I fling my arms around his neck. 'Thank you! Thank you! Thank you!'

'No worries,' he says, grabbing my wrists and disentangling himself with a grin. 'Give over, Kally, it's no big deal.'

But it was a big deal, it really was. D'you see what I mean about Jem? He can be the nicest person in the whole world if he wants to be. If he likes you.

And he obviously likes me.

A month later and the arrangement's working really well. Izzy loves being picked up by Jem two days a week; she can't wait for Mondays now. They do silly walks on the way home from school and tell each other corny jokes and I know for a fact Jem is teaching her rude rugby songs because I've heard her singing them to her Barbies. Then he waits with her till Mum gets home. I'm sharing my boyfriend with my kid sister. No, we're not sharing, she sees more of him than I do.

I'm not complaining, it's brilliant of him to help out. We couldn't manage without him. And what a change in Mum! Who would have thought a part-time job in a poxy little shop would make such a difference? She chats away about Pat and Geoff who run the garage and the store and all the customers as if I cared. Actually, I do, if it brings her back to normality.

Life's not so bad now. Mum's stopped being a zombie

and Megan's turning into a good mate. School's OK and I've got the best-looking boyfriend in the world and he's sooo nice to me. Yay!

Now all I want is my dad back.

I'm pretty sure Mum's in contact with him. Every so often she scuttles off to the phone box on the corner and comes back with puffy eyes and a red nose. But she never says anything and it's got like I don't feel I can ask. I'm not even sure when he's due out. I mean, I know he got three years but I've an idea he'll be out long before that because of things like parole and good behaviour. And my dad's bound to get that because he's so law-abiding.

How can you be law-abiding yet be banged up in prison for theft?

Because he didn't do it, that's why. He couldn't have. Not *my* dad.

I remember watching out for them to come home on the final day of the trial, through the front-room window. The last thing Mum did before they left for court in a taxi, all dressed up in their best clothes as if they were going to a wedding, was to place a bottle of champagne in the fridge. I saw her doing it and she winked at me and put her finger to her lips and said, 'Sshh!' so I knew it was going to be all right.

From what Mum had said, the trial was just a means of

clearing up all the misunderstanding and finding out where the money had gone. I knew for a fact that Dad's bank account had been frozen while they investigated, because one day Mum had come back from Tesco's beside herself with fury, having had to abandon a trolley-load of shopping at the checkout when her card refused to pay out. All through that horrible time she'd kept saying to Dad, 'The truth will come out at this bloody trial, don't you worry!' and he'd answer, 'Well, let's hope so,' but he didn't look too convinced because he'd run his hand through his hair when he said it which was always a sign he was worried.

So when the taxi drew up outside the house at last, I didn't wait to see them get out, I yelled, 'They're here!' and ran to get the champagne out of the fridge. Izzie and I stood in the hallway, me with my thumb poised to prise the cork out and Izzy with two glasses at the ready. The door opened and we yelled, 'SURPRISE!' and I popped the cork and the champagne shot out all over the carpet, but only Mum walked in.

Izzy said, 'Where's Dad?' and Mum got down to her knees and hugged her tight. I saw her face and it was soooo white and strained and my stomach constricted and I knelt down too and she put her arms round us both. And I remember the carpet was soaked from the champagne and my knees got wet.

'I want my daddy!' Izzy had wailed and that started me off because I wanted him too. Mum patted us both on the back, then she started crying as well, big, loud horrible sobs that racked up from deep inside her, and that made Izzy and me stop because it was frightening.

At last it was over and she blew her nose and sat back on her heels and looked at us and I swear she'd aged twenty years. Then she took a deep breath and said, 'You've got to be brave, girls. Daddy's gone abroad to work for a long time. But he *will* be back one day and until then we've got to get by on our own.'

My dad had been sent down (that's the term they use, as if they incarcerate all the prisoners in dungeons beneath the court) for a crime he didn't commit. I wanted to tell everyone it was all wrong, they'd made a big mistake, my dad wasn't a criminal, but Mum wanted to hush it all up. So to this day Izzy doesn't know he's in prison and I'm beginning to think my mother has forgotten *I* do, because she never talks about it. I don't even know where he is. Within days she'd put the house up for sale (maybe that had to go towards paying off the money that had disappeared, I don't know, she wouldn't say), packed our cases and the next thing we were on the train out of London to a new life in the country like three bewildered evacuees from the Second World War.

* * *

But it's not so bad here now I've got used to it. Apart from Whingy Walker, or the Dag as she's now been rechristened (oops, my fault that!), my teachers are fine. I don't know if she's aware of her new nickname or, worse still, she knows I'm responsible for it, but she's always on my case. Actually, I suspect it's because she knows I'm friends with Jem whom she hates with a vengeance. But I can take it, I've had worse to deal with than her gripes.

But now I'm playing netball, Megan and I are getting much closer which is ace. Though I know Megan doesn't like Jem. She hasn't said so, but I can tell; she keeps her distance. I wonder why? It's a shame, she should get to know him, then she'd realize what a cool guy he can be.

So, with this in mind, I start encouraging Megan and Holly and the others to sit around with us at lunchtimes. Jem's not too pleased at first, he'd rather have me to himself (flattering or what?), but he puts up with it, though I notice he hates it if he thinks I'm paying too much attention to any of the boys. One day we're on the field and Matt from my form is fooling about, doing this really over-the-top impression of the Dag, a cross between the Queen on a bad day and the Hunchback of Notre Dame, and everyone's rolling about laughing.

Everyone except Jem.

Suddenly Jem turns to me. 'Stop screeching,' he says coldly.

I gasp. 'I wasn't screeching. No more than anyone else.'

'He's not even funny,' he continues, with a scowl on his face.

'Yes he is!' I stare at him in surprise. 'Anyway, I thought you hated the Dag too.'

'Shit! When are you going to grow up!' He jumps to his feet.

'Jem?' I grab him by the arm but he shakes me off and slopes away. I watch him go, my mouth open in surprise.

'What was all that about?'

Megan frowns and shakes her head. 'He's jealous.'

'What of?'

'You, idiot. He can't stand you liking other boys.'

'Other boys?' The penny drops. 'I don't like Matt! Is that what you think?'

'That's what *he* thinks!'

'Flipping heck!' giggles Holly. 'He must be really keen or something.'

'Or something,' echoes Megan darkly.

There's no time to mull it over because the bell goes for afternoon school and we've got assembly followed by double Maths. Yuck! But when I come out of school, Jem is waiting for me. He's holding some flowers and has an apologetic smile on his face.

'I'm sorry I snapped at you.'

'That's OK.' I glance at the flowers. They're really nice

ones, red roses and pink and white lilies, the ones that smell really strong. But the stems are wet and they're not wrapped. 'Where did you get those from?'

He places them into my arms. 'The churchyard next door. I nipped out between lessons.'

'Jem! They're off someone's grave!' I thrust them back at him as if I've been burnt.

'Well, they're not going to miss them, are they?'

He hands them back to me. His face is irresistible, cheeky but plaintive at the same time. I giggle, despite myself.

'You are terrible!'

'I know. But that's the way you like me!' He puts his arm round me and plants a kiss on my nose just as Megan passes us. She raises her eyebrows but doesn't stop. There's a commotion going on at the bike sheds. A crowd gather round.

'What's going on?' I ask.

'Fight,' says Jem. 'Come on, let's go skating.'

As we pass, a few people start drifting away. 'What's up?' I call over.

'Someone's had their bike vandalized.'

'Who?'

'Matt,' says a voice at my elbow. It's Megan. 'Funny that, don't you think?'

* * *

On Saturday, I go to town with Mum. She's got a bit of extra money now from her job and she needs something new to wear to work (I can't begin to think why, nobody interesting comes into that grotty place), so she suggests a girly morning together looking round the shops. Well, I'm not going to say no to that, am I, especially if there's something in it for me? But also I'm pleased to see the old Mum coming back slowly, a bit like an old-style photograph emerging from a negative. So we drop Izzy off at Molly's and head for some serious retail therapy.

We have a great time. Mum chooses a couple of pretty tops and a new skirt and goes to try them on, then she calls me to see if they've got them in a smaller size. When I hand them to her in the changing room I realize how much weight she's lost with all the worry she's been through. She's not exactly skin and bone, but she's practically my size now, which is not really what you want your mum to be. In fact, from the back I reckon you could get us mixed up, because of our colouring. When did I grow into my mother?

After Mum's paid for her new gear we go into my sort of shops and Mum treats me to a new pair of jeans and a stripy top. We visit the toyshop next to choose something for Izzy and we deliberate over a stethoscope but it costs the earth. Then I have the brainwave of going to Boots and buying her a first-aid kit instead, which Mum thinks is a great idea though she says she'll have to take the scissors out before she plays with it.

After that I start thinking I'd better get back soon, because I've sort of got into a routine of meeting Jem to skate in the park for the past few Saturday afternoons. I'm wondering to myself if Mum will let me wear my new clothes (not if she knows I'm skating, she won't), when she says, 'Now, what about a spot of lunch?' She looks so bright-eyed and happy I haven't got the heart to say that I want to get off and anyway, I'm feeling peckish and I'm not going to turn down a free lunch out, am I? There's not many of those have come my way over the last few months.

So I say, 'Ace, Mum!' and I tuck my arm into hers and we walk down the High Street together chatting away nineteen to the dozen, with our bags in our hands, looking for somewhere to eat. And Mum says, 'What about there? That looks nice,' and points to a café across the road with a stripy awning and tables on the pavement and a blackboard advertising all the day's specials in neat white chalk writing, but with the apostrophes in all the wrong places.

I'm about to say yes, but my eyes light on a couple sitting together at a table in the window. They're deep in conversation and, as I watch, the boy leans towards the girl and says something in her ear and she bursts out laughing. They look as if they're getting on like a house on fire and, from this distance, you can't tell that the girl is older than the boy; you would only know that if you know them as well as I do.

'No,' I say, turning away. 'I don't fancy that one. I've just remembered, there's a good one down here,' and I lead her back the way we came and round the corner to the next street. It's not as nice but I don't care, I'm not hungry any more.

My appetite's gone.

Ever since I saw Jem chatting up Laura Baker.

I go to the park in the afternoon because I need to do something. 'See you later, Mum!' I yell and sneak off quickly before she's got a chance to see I'm in my new gear and I've got my board tucked under my arm. It's busy there, lots of young mums with buggies clogging up the pathways and little kids on bikes. There's no sign of Jem though. What a surprise.

My mind's in a turmoil. I'm gutted. Two voices argue with each other, relentlessly.

Your boyfriend's flirting with your kid sister's teacher! How could he do that? How could she? I mean, he's not even sixteen yet, it's illegal, isn't it?

But he's never actually said he's my boyfriend. I've kind of assumed that.

Yeah, but everyone else has too! You're a couple, the whole school knows that.

I know, I know. But you're letting your imagination

run away with you. You don't know they're up to anything.

No? Where is he then?

He'll be here in a minute.

Yeah, right. He's with her, you idiot. They're probably in her flat together this very minute.

My brain's rushing round in circles and my limbs start to follow it. I skate around the pathways, weaving my way through the mums and toddlers, building up speed, but I can't outrun the thoughts racing through my head. Laura Baker! Who does she think she is, with her big wide smile and trendy haircut? How dare she steal Jem! She's too old for him *and* she's a teacher! I'm going to report her to the authorities. She'll get locked up for years, serve her right!

My dad got locked up for years and he didn't do anything. Maybe she didn't do anything.

My wheels are moving faster and faster but they can't keep up with my mind, which is speeding ahead, and my head's down and I'm not looking where I'm going. All of a sudden there's a little kid in front of me; she's wearing cute pink jeans and she's bending over examining something on the ground, and it all happens in a flash. She's abandoned her trike on the path and I swerve to avoid it, and at the same time she straightens up and runs right in front of me. I jump off and go sprawling but the board smacks straight into her and knocks her flying. When I sit up she's on the ground and my mind registers weirdly, Izzy would love those pink jeans, but they're not cute any more, they've got dirt all over them and she starts bawling her head off. Her mother rushes to pick her up and yells at me too and, I can't help it, I burst into tears.

Soon there's a crowd around us, nearly all of them mums with little kids, saying things like, 'Better check her for broken bones,' and 'Take her to the hospital,' and 'It shouldn't be allowed!' and casting evil glances at me who's sitting up, sobbing my heart out and covered in dirt and snot, and no one offers to check my bones, even though my knee's throbbing and my head's hurting.

'I'm sorry,' I gulp, struggling to my feet and wiping my nose with the back of my hand. My new jeans are torn at the knee and my top is stained with earth and grass. 'Is she all right?'

'You shouldn't be skating in here!' snaps a woman who looks as if she'd like to string me up from the nearest lamppost. 'It's not allowed!'

'If she's seriously hurt, I'm holding you responsible,' yells the kid's mother. 'I want your name and address!'

'Call the police! There are signs all over the place saying no skateboarding. Lock them all up, I would!' spits another.

'I didn't mean it!' My eyes close momentarily, blotting out their angry faces, but it doesn't stop me from hearing their outrage, and darkness folds in on me. I sink back to the ground, dizzy with their hate, and hang my head between my knees. I wonder what Mum will do if a policeman comes to the door to tell her I've been arrested.

'Leave her alone!' My eyes snap open and I look up to see Jem, thrusting his way into the circle of venomous women surrounding me. 'Can't you see, she's hurt too.' He gets down on his haunches and puts his arms around me. 'Are you OK?' I nod, unable to speak, his concern making my tears flow again. The women quieten down, noticing for the first time my torn jeans and bleeding knee. One says kindly, 'You want to get that seen to, love. It needs cleaning up.'

Jem helps me to my feet and picks up my board. I put my weight on my leg and wince. 'I'm sorry,' I say again to the woman holding the little girl, quiet now in her arms. 'It was an accident.'

She sniffs. 'She'll be all right. But you shouldn't be skating in here. There's a sign there, can't you read?'

'The sign says no cycling too,' points out Jem quietly. The woman bristles.

'He's got a point, you know,' says the kind woman. 'There's nowhere for kids to play nowadays, big *or* small.'

'It's not right,' says one. 'The big ones need somewhere

to go too. Keep them off the streets.'

'You go and get that knee seen to,' says another. The mum puts the little girl back down and turns back to the other women and she toddles off again, forgotten. The trike remains upended on the path.

'Thanks,' I say to Jem as I hobble away, hanging on to his arm. 'I thought they were going to lynch me at first.'

'Can't leave you alone for a moment,' he grins. 'Look at the trouble you get into without me around to look after you.'

'Where were you?'

'Nowhere. Why?'

'I've been waiting for you for ages.'

'I went to town this morning, bought myself some new shoes. Like your gear, by the way.' He looks appreciatively at my new clothes.

'I've ruined them now. My mum will go spare. What else did you do?'

'Nothing much. Oh yeah,' his face brightens, 'you'll never guess who I had a coffee with.'

My heart beats faster. 'Holly?' I suggest innocently.

'No thanks!' He shudders. 'Miss Baker, Izzy's teacher. Laura.'

'Laura? Since when are you on first-name terms with teachers?'

He grins. 'She's not *my* teacher, is she? That's what she told me to call her.'

'Oh did she now? How come you're hobnobbing with her then on Saturday mornings?' My tone is light but I'm watching him like a hawk.

He shrugs. 'I just fancied a coffee and when I went in the café she was already sitting there. She said I could share her table because it was crowded, there were no free tables. She's nice.' He glances at me curiously. 'You don't mind, do you?'

'No, idiot.' I squeeze his arm happily. What am I like? All that angst for nothing. He's obviously got nothing to hide. Jem is kind and honest and reliable and loves me to bits and I should stop doubting him all the time, I'm no better than Megan or Mr Davey or the Dag. He's rapidly becoming my knight in shining armour and it's about time I started trusting him.

So, for that reason, when I'm lying in bed that night going over the events of the day, as you do, and I suddenly remember that the reason that I noticed Jem and Laura Baker in the first place was because they were sitting in splendid isolation in the window of an empty café, I tell myself to stop being paranoid, he was just protecting my feelings, and dismiss it from my mind.

* * *

The next day we have a visitor. The weather's rotten, cold and damp with that horrible low mist that hangs around here making you feel miserable, so Mum lights a fire for the first time in the small grate in the tiny front room. Izzy and I curl up in front of it, scorching our hands as we toast bread on forks. I have to hang on to her to stop her from pitching head-first into the burning logs. It's not very efficient, the bread curls up, burning black in places and staying virgin white in others but, smothered in butter, it's delicious.

When there's a *rat-tat-tat* at the door we look at each other in amazement. It's the first time anyone has knocked at our front door except for the postman, and today's Sunday. Izzy makes a dive to answer it.

'Hello. You must be Izzy. Is your mum in?'

It's a deep voice, male, pleasant and modulated, not the usual gruff burr of the local accent.

'Mum!' Izzy's voice has a touch of panic.

I stand up as Mum appears from the kitchen, wiping her hands on a towel. She looks as surprised as I do, but when she reaches the door her expression changes to a smile of recognition.

'Geoff! Come on in! Nice to see you.'

Geoff? Since when was my reclusive mum on first-name terms with strange men? A big bloke steps through the door, bending his head and twisting his shoulders to avoid the frame. When he straightens up he's not far off knocking his head against the beams. He's got tight grey curly hair and a full-on Father Christmas beard, grey dotted with swirls of white. Izzy gazes up at him, wide-eyed with awe.

'Geoff, these are my daughters, Kally and Izzy. Girls, this is Geoff, my new boss. He owns the garage and the shop where I work.'

'Good to meet you, Kally.' Geoff shakes hands with me first, then bends down to take Izzy's hand in his huge fist. 'Pleased to make your acquaintance, Izzy.'

She beams up at him. Me, I'm still reserving judgement.

'Nothing wrong, is there?' asks Mum.

'No, not at all. We just wondered if you could help us out. Is there any chance you could come in every day for the next fortnight? Run the store for us?'

Mum looks flustered. 'Oh, I don't know. I'd need to think about that.'

'I know it's short notice. But Pat wants to go back up to London to give our Josie a hand with the new baby. She's finding it all a bit overwhelming, I'm afraid.'

'I'd love to help,' says Mum. 'But there are arrangements I'd need to make. Izzy to pick up from school . . .'

'Jem can meet me,' says Izzy promptly.

Mum and I laugh. 'She's right, Mum. Jem and I can

manage between us. And we can lend a hand around the house, can't we, Izzy?'

Izzy nods importantly. 'I can make tea. I do my own breakfast now, when Mum has a lie-in.'

Mum looks embarrassed but Geoff doesn't appear to notice.

'I'd pay you manager's wages of course.'

'Go on, Mum.'

'Well . . . the money would come in handy, I have to admit. If you think I'm up to it . . .'

'Piece of cake! She's only been there two minutes and your mother's running that store with her eyes closed, Kally.'

I smile. Mum's face is shining. She looks like Cinderella being told she *can* go to the ball, not someone being offered two weeks' work in a back-of-beyond garage shop. She looks like Izzy.

'All right then, I'll do it! Two weeks, you say?'

'Two weeks. Thanks, Jan. I'll go and tell Pat to start packing. She'll be made up.'

'Thank *you*.'

'For what?'

'Placing your trust in me.'

'Oh I trust you all right. And that's another thing.' Geoff's eyes grow serious. 'While I'm up in London I'm going to pay a visit to my old office and look up the files on that case you were telling me about. There's more to it than meets the eye.'

'Thank you,' Mum whispers again. She looks as if she's going to cry. Geoff pats her arm.

'Bye, girls,' he smiles. 'Look after your mum. She's precious, you know.'

'Bye!' yells Izzy and stands at the door waving till Geoff strides off out of sight. 'I like Geoff,' she declares emphatically, slamming the door shut. She giggles. 'He said you're precious, Mum.'

'She is,' I say and Mum smiles at me. 'What was he on about, Mum? Going into his office and looking up files? I thought you said he owned the garage up the road.'

'He does now. But before he retired down here to run it, he was in the police force in London.'

My head snaps up. 'So what case is he going to look at?' Like I didn't know.

'Not now, Kally,' she says and turns away, and I'm really miffed. All that stuff about we mustn't tell anyone what's happened to Dad, we must keep it a secret, then the first person she talks to, she blurts it all out.

Still, it's nice to know there's someone on our side at last.

And it's good to see Mum back in control.

Immediately, Mum switches back into Super-Mum mode and washes and irons enough school uniform to keep us going for a month. Then she makes sandwiches for the morning, a lasagne for tomorrow's evening meal and, just as I'm going up to bed, gets the Hoover out 'to give the house a once-over'.

'Mum, for goodness' sake, you'll wake Izzy. Anyway, there's no need.'

'There's every need. I don't want the house going to rack and ruin because I'm working full time,' says Mum, brandishing the vacuum hose. 'Out of my way, Kally.'

'Think about it! Now you're a busy career woman and out of the house all day, there's no one here to see the mess, is there? Get real, Mum. You'll be exhausted before you start.'

'Oh dear, I suppose you're right,' says Mum collapsing on the sofa. 'You're so good at bringing me back down to earth, Kally.' Her face falls. 'Busy career woman, my foot. Working in a garage shop. It's not much of a job, is it?'

'It's a start. And you're the manager now for a while, remember? I'm proud of you, Mum.' I drop a kiss on the top of her head. 'And so will Dad be, when you tell him.'

It's the first time I've acknowledged I know she's in communication with Dad. She turns to face me and grabs my hand. 'He's proud of *you*, Kally. It's what keeps him going, hearing how you and Izzy are getting on with your lives.' She hesitates, then she adds quietly, 'He's pleased to hear you're skating again.'

I *so* want to ask her loads of questions like,

Where is he?

and

When's he coming out?

and

He'll come to live with us when he does, won't he?

and

Why's he in there in the first place?

and

What really happened, Mum?

But it's enough for now that she's talked about him. She pats my hand and says, 'Night night, love,' and closes her eyes and I know she's not going to give any more. I've just got to bide my time till she's ready.

* * *

It all works out OK. Jem picks up Izzy as usual on Monday and stays with her till I get home from netball practice. She's upstairs playing in our bedroom with her new first-aid kit. Barbies are strewn all round the room, dressed in impressive bloodstained bandages. Obviously there's been a major incident, but luckily Dr Isobel O'Connor has everything under control.

'Gory!' I observe appreciatively as I take in the disaster area.

'Tomato sauce,' explains Jem. He's sitting at my desk doing some homework. I glance involuntarily at my diary which I'd left out on the desk the night before. He's pushed it to one side to make room. I'm not quite comfortable with this. I mean, he could pick it up and discover all my secrets.

Like how I feel about him!

And how I feel about what's happened to my dad.

He glances up at me and gives me his special lopsided smile. My heart melts. Jem's not going to do that, is he? Of course he isn't. Trust, Kally. Trust.

Even so, I resolve to put my diary away from now on.

'Thanks for looking after her. Want to watch TV for a bit? Or I've got a DVD free with my new skating magazine, we could have a look at that?'

'Sorry, I've got loads of stuff to do tonight for

school.' He scoops his work off my desk and sweeps it into his bag. This is seriously unlike Jem. He catches my look of surprise and his lip curls in self-derision. 'I know, it's a pain. But the Dag said if I don't get my essay in, I'm in detention tomorrow night. And we can't have that, can we? I've got a job to do. I've got Izzy to meet from school.'

He holds up his hand to give her a high-five. Her face breaks into a delighted smile as she reaches up to slap his hand then returns to tending her wounded patients. 'See you tomorrow, Jem,' she says, dismissing him, safe in the complete assurance that he'll be there for her the next day.

'You bet,' he says and pauses as he looks at me. His eyes are serious and just for a second I wonder if he'll kiss me. Almost imperceptibly, I can feel my body leaning towards his and my eyes starting to close as I think, THIS IS IT! But then he says, 'You too, Kally,' and my eyes shoot open wide and I say, 'Yeah, see you, Jem,' as he touches my arm and squeezes past me.

After he's left I throw myself on the sofa to watch telly but my mind goes walkabout again.

Why doesn't he kiss me? Doesn't he like me?

Of course he does, he's going home early to get his homework done so tomorrow he can pick up your little sister for you, idiot! This is Jem, school rebel, who doesn't give a toss about anyone. Except you.

So why doesn't he kiss me then?

I need to talk to someone about this, someone real instead of the irritating voice in my head. But who? I can't ask Mum, she's got enough to deal with herself and, anyway, I'd be too embarrassed. I can't ask Megan because she doesn't like Jem and I can't ask Holly because she likes him too much.

Maybe I need to talk to Jem himself.

But the next day, when Jem gets on the bus, he has his dark, moody face on.

'What's up?' I ask, but he mutters, 'Nothing,' and stares morosely out of the window.

After a while I ask tentatively, 'Did you get your essay done?' I can't bear the silent treatment.

'Nope.' Then he adds, viciously, 'Don't worry, I'll pick Izzy up all right. You can go to your precious netball training.'

'Jem! I didn't mean that!'

He has the grace to look shamefaced. 'No, I'm sorry, I don't suppose you did.'

'What's wrong?' I slip my hand into his. 'Is it something at home?' He shakes his head. It occurs to me that I know zilch about Jem's home life. I don't even know where he lives. 'Can I help?'

He sighs and squeezes my hand. 'You do help,' he says. He turns to look at me with his beautiful brown eyes and for a moment he looks sooo vulnerable. 'You don't know how much it means that you are here for me.'

'I always will be,' I say and squeeze his hand in return.

At lunchtime, we're sitting under the covered area by the canteen, a crowd of us, when the Dag comes bearing down towards us. She stops in front of Jem and presents him triumphantly with a red detention slip.

'That essay should have been on my desk, nine o'clock this morning, Jermaine. Two-hour detention tonight, my room.'

'You can't,' I protest. 'You have to give twenty-four hours' notice.'

'I warned him yesterday, thank you, Kally,' she snaps. 'Don't try to tell me how to do my job.'

Jem takes the piece of paper with a sneer. 'Yippee,' he says casually and tucks it into his shirt pocket. He treats her to his contemptuous smile. 'It's a date. I'll look forward to it, *Mrs* Walker.'

The kids around us titter nervously. The Dag looks as if she wants to wipe the smile off his face with the flat of her hand but she turns on her heel and marches away instead. I sigh deeply.

'I'd better go and tell Miss Morgan I can't make netball practice. She's not going to like this.'

Jem places his hand on my arm. 'Not so fast. It may not

come to that.'

'What do you mean?'

'Well,' he does his lazy grin this time, 'don't jump the gun. Anything could happen between now and the end of the afternoon.'

'Jem? What are you up to?'

He spreads his hands wide and assumes a look of innocence. 'Me? Nothing.' Then his expression changes. 'I told Izzy I'd pick her up and *I* don't break my word. Not like some people.'

He looks so serious it's scary. Everyone falls silent. When the bell goes, people jump up as if they're relieved to be away. I leave Jem sitting there in a world of his own, playing games on his phone.

I'm in English, first period of the afternoon, sitting near the front, when one of the office staff, the one with the cleavage, comes in with a message for the Dag. She says, 'I'm sorry, Mrs Walker, I'm afraid it's an emergency.' My ears prick up; this is far more interesting than preparing for SATs, but she whispers to the Dag and her words are lost.

The Dag's face isn't though. She blanches. You read about this in books all the time, though you'd never think it was possible. But I know it is because I saw Mum's face turn white when she came back from court, so I know it's really bad news and I tense up.

She picks up her bag and says, 'Sorry, class, I'm afraid I've got to go,' and everyone looks at her in amazement because she does sound genuinely sorry. Then she rushes out and Megan says, 'What's happened, Miss?' and the secretary answers, 'Her husband's had a heart attack. It's serious.'

And then she adds, 'Oh dear, I probably shouldn't have told you that. Just get on with your work.'

We look at each other, then we do as we're told, because I suppose everyone's thinking, like I am, how awful it must be to suddenly hear that the person you love, the one person in the world surely, in the Dag's case, is about to die.

And even though I don't like her, I feel unbearably sad. We must all be feeling the same because we file out of class at the end of the lesson in silence.

Outside Jem is waiting for me.

'It's OK, Kal,' he says. 'You go to netball practice, I'll collect Izzy.'

'What about your detention?' I ask.

He winks at me. 'Sorted,' he says.

The next day when we get to school, all the talk in the classroom is about Mrs Walker's husband. Weirdly, she's returned to her rightful name. It seems disrespectful to call her the Dag in the circumstances.

'I bet you anything he's dead,' says Holly. 'Some bloke had a heart attack in the shopping centre a few weeks ago and he died. It was on a Saturday morning, everyone saw it, he was frothing at the mouth apparently. His wife must have been well embarrassed.'

'You don't always die when you have a heart attack,' says Darren. 'My granddad's had loads.'

'Your granddad would,' says someone else and we all laugh.

'She won't be back for a while, that's the main thing,' says Matt and the conversation turns to who we'll have instead. I glance at Megan. She's at her desk, copying out some homework, taking no part in the discussion.

'D'you know anything about it?' I ask. She shakes her head and hunches over her work. I can tell she does. I bet her dad's told her what's going on.

I always get the sense that Megan knows a lot more about school stuff than she lets on. It stands to reason, he talks to her, there's only the two of them at home. But Megan's not a gossip, she keeps it all to herself. It's lucky for Mr Davey that Holly's not his daughter, otherwise nobody in the school would be able to keep anything secret.

Including me.

I wonder, not for the first time, if Megan knows about my dad being in prison.

Nah, what was it Mr Davey said on my first day? 'Nobody except the Head and myself is aware of what's happened. And that's the way it will stay.'

I trust Mr Davey. You know when you can trust someone, don't you? And, let's face it, she probably wouldn't be friends with me if she knew. She'd give me the cold shoulder, like Ella did.

She cold-shoulders Jem. I wonder what she knows about him?

Suddenly the door opens and Mrs Walker walks in. I'm sitting on a desk but I jump up in surprise. She looks pale but otherwise normal.

'Hurry up and sit down, the bell's gone,' she barks at

the class and we obey quickly. She opens her laptop to take the register, scanning the classroom to locate people as we sit in silence. After a while, Holly puts her hand up.

'Yes?'

'Is your husband all right, Miss?'

'Yes thank you, he's perfectly all right.'

'But I thought . . .' Holly's voice trails away. Everyone is staring at Mrs Walker, waiting for her to speak. At last she closes the laptop, folds her arms and looks at us.

'You thought he'd had a heart attack?'

We nod. 'Yes, Miss.' Surely she wouldn't have come to school if he'd died? He must be all right.

'So did I.' She gives a big sigh and looks out of the window before focusing back at us and shaking her head. 'It was a hoax. Someone's idea of a joke.'

A gasp goes round the classroom.

'That's sick, Miss.'

Megan voices what everyone's thinking. A buzz of conversation begins and builds up in momentum, I can hear their voices in the background, sharp with disbelief and indignation, but I take no part in it. I've gone cold and still and I can hear a much, much louder voice drumming inside my own skull, saying over and over again.

Sorted. Sorted. Sorted. Sorted.

I'm suddenly aware Mrs Walker is fixing me with her

cold stare and, unable to meet her eyes, I look down at my desk. But I hear what she says.

'The matter is under full investigation, so if you don't mind, I don't want to hear any more about it. Now hurry up or you'll be late for your first lesson.'

Without looking up, I grab my bag and head for the door.

At breaktime I search for Jem but he's nowhere to be seen. It's the same at lunchtime, but by then I know where he is. Word's got round that he's sitting outside Mr Davey's office with some other choice individuals of whom he's the primary suspect for the hoax. By this time it's the talk of the school.

'I bet it was Jem,' says Holly admiringly. 'He's the only person who would dare pull a stunt like that.'

'It's not clever, Holly,' says Megan. 'It's horrible.'

'You don't know it's Jem!' I protest. 'It could be anyone.'

'It's a bit of a coincidence, Kally, you've got to admit,' Matt butts in. 'He wanted to get out of his detention, it's obvious.'

'Only because he had to pick up my sister for me!' I bite my lip.

'So it *was* him! I knew it was!' Holly looks positively delighted.

'Were you in on it?' asks Darren in surprise.

'No of course I wasn't! I mean, you don't know he did it, you can't prove it. It could have been anyone!'

'They've traced the call to his mobile, Kally.'

'How do you know that?' I stare at James in horror as he flops down beside us on the grass.

'I've just spoken to Sam. They've let him and the others go. Jem's with Mr Davey and the Head now.'

I look at the circle of faces round me. Holly's is bright with interest. She's loving this. Darren looks disgusted, Matt looks upset and Megan won't look at me at all. I feel like screaming at them, it's not my fault!

Déjà vu. Day Sha Voo. I've been here before.

'He didn't do it.' I get to my feet. 'He's not like that.'

Megan ignores me. I yell at her, 'I'm going to sort this out! He wouldn't do it! He wouldn't!' She turns away and I stand for a moment, impotent with rage, then march off towards the Head's office. As I get there, the door opens and Jem comes out, his bag over his shoulder. He winks at me and a wave of relief passes over me, so strong it makes me feel faint. Behind him, Mr Davey stands in the door, looking grim. His voice booms. 'The bell's about to go. Get to your lesson, Jermaine.'

Jem turns. 'Yeah, I wouldn't want to be late, would I? Not now I've missed all my lessons this morning.'

Mr Davey slams the door.

'What happened?'

Jem puts his arm round my shoulder. 'Couldn't prove a thing.'

'But they traced the call to your mobile!'

Jem's eyebrows arch. 'Kally! You didn't think I made that call, did you? I'm surprised at you. I thought you had more faith in me than that.'

I'm flustered. I don't know what to believe. I feel caught like a fish on a line. Jem reels me in.

'It was my mobile all right. But I lost it yesterday lunchtime. Luckily I went to report it missing at the office at afternoon registration. So, as I pointed out to them, whoever stole it made the call.' He shook his head. 'You can't trust anyone nowadays, Kally. There are a lot of villains about.'

I stare at him. His tone is mocking but his eyes are wide, innocent. I take a deep breath.

'Was it you, Jem?'

'I just told you, my phone was pinched. I thought you said you'd always be there for me?'

'I will! I am! But Jem, I need to know the truth.'

He stares down at me. I can feel myself being drawn up into his gaze. Then he kisses me gently. At last.

As he draws away, he says quietly,

'Kally, I would never lie to you.'

I've waited a long time for this moment and it's magic.

Later in bed I play the scene over and over in my head

and as I drift off to sleep I can feel the pressure of Jem's lips on mine.

That night I dream crazy, whirling dreams where people chase each other in circles and do weird, staccato dances, as if they were puppets. The Dag's there, tossing a pile of red detention slips in the air, and Laura Baker's chopping them up with her scissors as they fall to the ground; the bald man is driving his car and crashing it into Matt's bike and Darren's jumping up and down on his skateboard. They're all whizzing around at breakneck speed, then, as I watch, they slow down and collapse before they jerk upright and zoom off again. In the middle, Jem sits, peacefully pressing buttons on his mobile phone. When I look closer I can see that it's Jem who's controlling the pace, controlling them, like an electronic puppet-master, making them go fast or slow, stand up, fall down. Then I see I'm there too, on my skateboard, and he's controlling me as well.

When I wake up I'm covered in sweat and my heart's racing as if I'm still in the dream. I lie there, allowing the tide of panic to wash over me until I cool down and it recedes like waves on a shore.

And it's then, as my heartbeat returns to normal and my mind clears and I remember Jem's kiss, I realize that Jem had avoided answering my question.

'What you doing after school?'

'Picking up Izzy. Why?'

'Never mind. Just wondered if you wanted to do something. Go to town. Have a coffee. Hang out . . .'

'I'd love to!' This was an opportunity I didn't want to miss. Megan had been funny with me since the Dag episode, not horrible, but sort of distant. I glance around the playground. 'Where's Jem? He'll get her for me, I'm sure. He's good like that.'

'He'll do anything for you. You're a good influence on him, Kally.'

I smile at her in delight. From Megan this was a compliment indeed. It's rare she's got a good word to say about Jem. Actually, it's rare anyone's got a good word to say about him, to be honest. He hangs around with me in school but I can tell other people are wary of him, they kind of avoid him. I've noticed Matt and Darren tend to take themselves off after a while when he appears and I put that down at first to the skateboard and bike incidents, even though neither of them was really Jem's fault. But other people do it too. It's just the airhead girls like Holly and those who are drawn to him, because he's so good-looking and they don't get it when he insults them.

Does that make me an airhead too?

It would be good to talk to Megan. She's an individual and I respect her judgement. I want to talk to her about Jem. I'm all mixed up about him. There are so many things I love about him. For instance,

- his looks
- his skateboarding skills
- his funny side (though sometimes he can be a bit cruel)
- his devotion to me
- his lopsided smiles
- his kisses.

But there are also things I don't like about him. For example,

- his possessiveness
- his moodiness
- his secrecy (though this does also make him mysterious which is kind of exciting)

- the way he always has to get his own back.

I spot Jem over by the bike shed. He's on his mobile, a new one. The other one never turned up. When he hangs up he's scowling but I call out to him and he comes over.

'Everything all right?' I ask. Now I'm getting to know Jem better, I'm starting to be able to read him. If you think about it people are a lot like books, only instead of just going by the words they say, you can read lots of other stuff, like the tone of their voices, gestures, body language, facial expressions, etcetera, to tell you what's going on. In Jem's case, I need to do this. He doesn't tell me much about himself, you see. He's a very private person.

'Yep,' he says, but I know it isn't because his eyebrows are drawn together in a frown and his voice is clipped. (See what I mean?) He leans against the wall beside me. 'What d'you want?'

'Would you mind picking up Izzy for me? I know it's my turn but . . .'

'No problem.' He brightens up visibly. 'Your wish is my command.'

Jem's willingness to please me is flattering. Especially in front of Megan.

'I'm going to town for a coffee with Megan,' I say, by way of explanation. 'Girly chats.'

Jem hesitates and for a moment I think he's going to change his mind. But he says, 'That's OK. Take your time.'

Under her breath Megan mutters, 'I'm impressed,' and I'm glad she's starting to see Jem in a better light, but then the moment's ruined because her dad appears by the staffroom entrance and yells, 'Jermaine! A word.' We watch as Jem saunters over to him and even from here we know it's not good news.

You can tell there's an argument going on because Jem shakes his head and you can hear his voice raised which is rare for him. Then Mr Davey loses his rag and lets rip and Jem takes his hands out of his pockets and straightens up, which he's obviously been told to do, and stares defiantly into the distance. Finally, as Mr Davey disappears back indoors, Jem slopes back to us with a face like thunder and says, 'Sorry, ladies, you'll have to forget about your girly chat, the pillock's put me in detention.'

'Jem, don't say that!' I look at Megan. She's as still as a statue and in profile, but her face is aflame. I know how awful it is to have your father called names. Megan pushes herself away from the wall with her foot and goes off without a word.

The bell goes and everyone files into school but I ignore it. I'm furious at Jem.

'Now look what you've done!'

He stands there, his face drawn tight with anger.

I take a deep breath.

'What's he put you in detention for, anyway? Isn't he supposed to give you notice?'

'Yeah, that's what I said! But it's the ******* one I should have done ages ago for the Dag. I thought they'd ******* forgotten about it.' He carries on cursing out loud, his face contorted in fury, and takes a savage kick at a stone. It hits one of the staff cars.

'Stop it!' I shout. 'I hate it when you act like this!'

In answer he slams his fist against the wall and I jump back in shock. He's missed me by inches. He tucks his hand under his armpit immediately. He's hurt himself, it's obvious, his eyes are closed and his face is drained of colour. I touch his arm.

'Are you all right?'

He whimpers with pain. I take his hand and inspect it gently. The knuckles are torn and bleeding but I can move the fingers so I don't think anything's broken.

'Jem? What have you done?'

'I'm sorry, Kally, I'm sorry.'

He's crying now, with pain I guess, but I'm not sure. I put my arms round him.

'It's OK, don't worry, it's OK. I'm here.'

'Don't leave me, Kally. You won't leave me, will you?'

'Of course I won't.'

'You'll get fed up with me soon like everyone else,' he

sobs. 'Everyone leaves me in the end.' I hold him in my arms and pat his back automatically, like I'm comforting Izzy, and say firmly, 'Well I'm not going to,' but actually, the truth is, I want to run away. I'm horrified. This can't be Jem, big, confident, scary Jem who doesn't give a damn about anyone.

Except me.

'I wanted to pick Izzy up for you and now I can't.' His voice is distraught. He sounds like a small child, broken with grief because he's had a beloved toy taken away from him for being naughty.

'It doesn't matter, honest! It's not important. I can go!'

I have to lighten this. It's far too heavy for me. 'Anyway, I think Megan might have changed her mind. I don't think she wants to go for a coffee with me any more.' I give him a rueful grin and he wipes his eyes and gives me a watery smile back.

'You think I'm an idiot, don't you?'

'No. I just think you've got a foul temper and you don't like not getting your own way.' I giggle, 'Listen to me. I sound like your mother.'

His face darkens. 'No you don't.' He looks into my eyes. 'I'm sorry, Kally. Forgive me?'

I kiss him gently on the nose. 'It's Megan you should apologize to, not me.'

'I don't care about her, I care about you.'

'Just do it! For me! Look, Jem, I'm late for French. You'd better go and get that seen to.'

He shrugs. 'It's OK now, it's gone numb,' but he moves off towards the office and I make my way to the Languages Block. Just as I'm going in through the door he calls to me.

'Thanks, Kally.' Then he adds, 'You're the one person who understands me.'

I wave and turn away with a sigh. Actually, Jem, I'm not too sure that I do. Being Jem's girlfriend can be a bit of a double-edged sword.

I really want to put it right with Megan. She manages to avoid speaking to me during lessons but I grab her arm as she goes to disappear out of the door at the end of the afternoon and force her to turn and face me.

'Look, I'm sorry, Jem shouldn't have said that. He was way out of order.'

Megan eyes me coldly as if I'm some disgusting specimen on a slab in the Science room. I can't bear it, I need her friendship. I start to gabble.

'He doesn't mean it, Megan, it's just when he loses his temper. He was sorry afterwards. You know, he can be really nice and kind when you get to know him, it's just a front he puts up . . .'

She shakes her head. 'You're too good for him, Kally. He's a nasty piece of work.'

'No he's not.' I stare at her, stung to the quick. 'You've seen what he's like, he'd do anything for me, you said so yourself. He puts me first.'

'He puts himself first. Always.' She walks away.

I shout after her. 'You don't know him!'

Megan calls back over her shoulder. 'Neither do you! Get rid, Kally.'

Holly, who's taking it all in, starts to giggle. I'm livid, but short of grabbing her thin mousy hair and knotting it round her fat throat, there's nothing I can do. She runs after Megan and takes her arm but at least I have the satisfaction of seeing Megan shake it off. She's her own person, Megan.

I always thought I was too.

There's no time to dwell on it or I'll be late to collect Izzy. I run to the main gate only to see the bus disappearing in the distance. Blast! I'm going to have to leg it.

By the time I get to the primary school, everyone's gone home. Izzy's sitting forlornly in the entrance hall on her own, clutching her bag. She springs up when she sees me and beams with relief.

'Kally! Where have you been? I've been waiting for ages!'

'Where is everyone? Have they all gone home and left you?' I'm astounded. I can't believe teachers would leave a six-year-old alone. 'Where's Miss Baker?'

'She's in the classroom. She's busy. She asked me who was coming to collect me and I said I forgot but I thought it might be Jem, so she told me to wait outside till he came for me.' Izzy sniffed. 'I don't like waiting by myself, Kally.'

Oh dear. It sounds like Miss Baker's got fed up with babysitting after hours. I'm surprised all the same. She seemed so nice the first time I met her and she was the one who said not to worry if I was ever late, she'd look after Iz. I don't call this looking after my little sister, forcing her to sit out here alone.

I grab Izzy by the hand, pick up her bag and push the classroom door open. Miss Baker is at the far end of the classroom, putting up a display on the wall, her back to us, but I can tell she's heard us come in because she freezes and then she says, coldly and clearly, without turning round, 'I've told you before, you're not to come into this classroom. You've no right. I'll call the caretaker if necessary. He's still on the premises.'

Izzy and I stand there, hand in hand, rooted to the spot. I'm confounded. That's no way to talk to a six-year-old! Iz looks up at me, her little face confused, then Miss Baker turns round and her hand goes to her mouth and she says, 'Oh, it's you, Kally! I'm so sorry, I thought you were someone else!' Her face is flushed now with embarrassment and she blethers, trying to cover up and make out everything's normal. 'Have you got everything, Izzy? Good girl. She's doing so well, Kally. She's got a new reading book, haven't you, Izzy?'

'I'm sorry I'm late, I missed the bus.'

'Oh, that's all right, she's no trouble, only . . . I had to get on with my work, you see . . .'

Her voice breaks off, then she whispers, 'I'm sorry,' and looks down as if she's going to cry and I go towards her but she backs away and puts her palms up towards me as if she wants to push me away and says, 'No, I'm fine. Been a long day.' She gives us a twisted little smile and says, 'See you tomorrow, Izzy,' and turns away.

I hold the door open for Izzy and say, 'Bye, Miss, thank you,' and suddenly she turns around.

'Kally?' she says. 'Who will be collecting Izzy from now on?'

I think for a minute. Netball training has finished for the season and Geoff and Pat are home next week so Mum will be back to working two days again. 'It'll be me Mondays and Tuesdays and Mum the rest of the week,' I calculate. 'I'll try not to be late.'

She nods and smiles widely, showing her perfect teeth.

The funny thing is, this time her smile reminds me of Izzy's when I'd walked into the school five minutes earlier. It's one of relief.

People are never what they seem to be, are they? So much has happened I'm lost in thought on the way home. Jem, in a temper, well I've seen that before, but crying like that! This is a new Jem for me and I'm not sure what to think. And the way he reacted when I said I was like his mother! What was all that about? Or did I imagine it?

And then what about Miss Baker acting weird? I wonder why she was so nervous and upset? It was as if she was scared to death of someone. Someone she works with perhaps? I wonder what's going on there?

I'm starting to feel I'm the only sane one around here. I've got so much to think about, it takes me a while to realize that Izzy is trailing behind me, unusually quiet, dragging her bag on the ground.

'What's up, Iz-Wiz?' I ask, tugging her plait.

'Kally,' she says, looking up at me dolefully, 'I don't think Miss Baker likes me any more.'

'Of course she does!' I come to a full stop and crouch down on the pavement beside her, gripping her by the arms so I can see her sad little face. 'Why do you think that, silly?'

She sniffs and her bottom lip juts out, a sure sign that she's close to tears.

'She said, "Oh, here we go again!" when everyone had gone today and it was just me left, and she looked really cross. Then she said she had lots of work to do and I had to be ready for Jem and sit outside.'

'She's just busy, Iz. She wasn't being mean.'

'Yes she was. I don't like her any more. She was mean to Jem yesterday when he came to collect me.'

'Was she?' I stare at her in surprise. 'He never said.'

'Jem wanted to chat but she wouldn't talk to him. She told him to go away and stop bothering her.'

'That's not very nice!' Poor Jem. No wonder he thinks no one likes him. He didn't deserve that, just for being friendly.

'She doesn't like talking to anyone,' continued Izzy. 'Today her phone was ringing in her bag at lunchtime and I told her but then she wouldn't answer it.'

'She's working too hard. Stress. That's what teachers suffer from. It's quite common.' I give Izzy a hug. 'Tell you what! I'll let you bandage me up when we get home.'

Her face lights up. 'Promise?'

'Promise. Come on, give us your bag.'

We continue home, hand in hand. Izzy's done it again, transferred all her worries on to me, and now she skips by my side, happy as Larry. (Who *is* Larry by the way?) I wish *I* was six and my big sister could make everything right for me. Instead I'm fourteen and bowed down with bags, the prospect of being bandaged and my own private burdens.

Jem and I are becoming closer. We're more open with each other now. I caught a glimpse of the real Jem that day, beneath the cool, disdainful exterior he presents to the rest of the world, and I saw a hurt little boy who's scared stiff of being abandoned.

Only, I don't mean to be harsh, but sometimes he's not very lovable. Most days he seems to rub someone up the wrong way. It's usually teachers, but not always.

Like, what he did to Holly, it was cruel.

But like he said, she asked for it. Perhaps he's right. Maybe she did need teaching a lesson.

But did he have to take such drastic action?

Anyway, what happened was, this particular day she turned up at school in a new, off-the-shoulder, definitely not regulation, black school jumper over her school shirt. The Dag, predictably, told her to take it off but then at lunchtime she put it back on again. We were out on the school field and suddenly she squealed, 'Oh, I'm too hot in this!' but instead of taking her jumper off she undid the buttons of her school shirt and wriggled out of it and lay down to sunbathe in her little black off-the-shoulder number, showing off her fake tan and leaving little to the imagination. And everyone ignored her.

So after a while she sat up and started flirting with Jem and you could see she was getting on his nerves.

'Take my picture on your new phone, Jem,' she pleaded. 'I want to see what I look like in my new top.'

'Like a slapper,' muttered Megan and I giggled but then, to my surprise, I realized that Jem was doing as he's told for once in his life and he was snapping away to Holly's delight, encouraging her to pull the jumper down even further.

'I feel like a model!' she simpered. Her poses were becoming more and more provocative and Jem was encouraging her to pout at the camera and suddenly I couldn't stand it any more, so I stalked off to the girls' toilets where, I couldn't help it, I dissolved into a blubbing wreck. How could he?

By the time Megan came to find me I'd got it together and was rinsing my face in cold water. She put a sympathetic arm round my shoulders and I shook it off before I started howling again.

'Take no notice,' she said. 'Jem's not interested in Holly, he's just doing it to shut her up.'

There were no towels so I stuck my face under the warm-air dryer and hoped that would explain its blotchy red appearance. 'He looks interested to me,' I said gruffly.

I was so hurt.

'Don't upset yourself, Kal. It's you he likes, anyone can see that.'

How ironic was that, Megan sticking up for Jem?

'He's got a funny way of showing it.'

She shrugs. 'You know me, I'm not exactly his number one fan. But I do know he doesn't like Holly and he's mad about you.'

Impulsively I hug her. 'Thanks. You're a mate.' It's good to have someone who cares.

That afternoon I found out what Jem's game was.

We were in IT when Darren, who was next to me, suddenly let out a roar. 'Get an eyeful of this, guys!' The boys clustered round his computer and there were lots of chuckles and crude comments and we girls raised our eyebrows and got on with what we were supposed to be doing, all except for Holly who couldn't resist going over to have a peep. It all went quiet then, and I looked up to see her staring at the screen goggle-eyed, then she shrieked and ran out of the room. The teacher came rushing over, telling everyone to sit down and demanding to know what site Darren was on.

'Just the intranet, Sir,' he said innocently. 'Look!'

Despite myself, I glanced over and grabbed an eyeful of Holly in all her glory. It was a head and shoulders photograph of her: she was staring dewy-eyed into the lens and her lips were pursed into a kiss and it looked as if she had nothing on. On the bottom of the picture, just covering her breasts, was the slogan 'STANFORD TECHNOLOGY COLLEGE, SLAG OF THE YEAR' in bold black capitals.

I knew when that photograph was taken. Lunchtime. She wasn't in the nude at all. Jem had encouraged her to pull her jumper low and off the shoulders and now it looked as if she was revealing all of her voluptuous charms, her modesty only protected by the savage slogan.

And now he'd posted it on the school website for everyone to gawp at. It had to be him.

At least he didn't deny it. Not to me, anyway.

'Why did you do it?' I ask, appalled, on the way home that night.

'She's in my face all the time! She knows I'm going out with you but she's all over me like a rash. I did it to show her once and for all I'm not interested.'

'Yeah, but Jem, that's no way to do it! I feel sorry for her.'

He snorts in derision.

'I do! I mean, everyone knows she's a flirt and yeah, she went too far but she's just . . . annoying. She didn't mean any harm.'

'Yeah, well neither did I. So we're quits.'

We walk on in silence. I can feel the tension radiating from him. It's our first proper argument.

'You could have got into real trouble, Jem, if she'd split on you.'

He shrugs. 'It worked, didn't it?'

It worked all right. She's avoiding Jem like the plague and me as well. Like I'm tarred with the same brush. Not a nice feeling.

I can't let him get away with this. I take a deep breath.

'That was a nasty, cruel thing to do, Jem. I hate it when you act like this.'

He stops dead and stares at me in surprise. 'You don't get it, do you? I did it for you.'

'For me?'

'Yeah. She upset you, didn't she?'

'*You* upset me!'

'She was trying to make you look stupid.'

'No she wasn't! She was making herself look stupid!'

He's silent for a minute then he says, 'I've cocked up again, haven't I?' He peers at me through his fringe, his lower lip jutting out, like a small boy who's been chastised, and I can feel myself softening towards him. But then he spoils it by adding, 'Why are we arguing about a stupid little slut like Holly anyway?'

'Don't call her that! It's horrible!'

'What?' He looks startled.

'Slut! Slag! Listen to yourself. It's arrogant and . . . vile and . . . a terrible way to talk about girls!' I'm surprised how strongly I feel, me who mentally labelled Holly a tart, but it's different somehow, it's like he's making out she's something sordid and loathsome and she's not, she's just stupid and she needs someone to stick up for her.

'I've done it again, haven't I?' His face crumples. 'Don't be mad at me, Kally. I'm sorry, I don't mean it.'

His voice breaks. I reach out my hand and he grabs it tight. 'I just get so mad when someone annoys me.' He takes a deep breath. 'I find it so hard to control my temper, it frightens me sometimes. I'm not proud of it, Kally.'

He looks wretched. It's big of him to admit his failings. My exasperation dissipates.

'Come here,' I say and give him a hug.

'Will you help me, Kal?' he asks pathetically. 'Can we work on this together?'

I nod. How could I refuse? His face breaks into a smile. 'I don't deserve you, Kally.'

The thing is, I know he means it. When he looks me

straight in the eye like that, I know he's telling the truth. Because, for all his swaggering ways, he's so insecure underneath. I keep thinking about what Megan said, about how I'm a good influence on him, and I'm sure I can help him change, learn to control his temper, be a nicer person.

Because he is nice, deep down, honest he is.

Since the Holly incident, people have tended to give us a wide berth. We're now an official couple and we spend all the time we can in each other's company. Jem's quite possessive, you know. He doesn't like sharing me with anyone else. Gone are my Saturday afternoon jaunts to town with the girls: he's put a stop to those because he wants to be with me. I don't mind, not really.

We skate a lot which is brilliant. I've come on so much under his direction; Dad'll be amazed when he comes out. Or we take the bus and go further afield, getting to know the surrounding area which is new to both of us. Once we even went as far as the coast and skimmed stones into the sea and walked along the beach hand in hand. It was so romantic, like we were in a film or something. He took loads of photos of me on my own and then some of us together, with his phone held at arm's length, but our faces looked fat and squashed up because we were too close to the lens.

Actually, it's not really true he doesn't want anyone else around. He doesn't mind Izzy so sometimes we take her with us. Jem's got more patience with her than I have, strange that; he doesn't mind her chatting all the time, in fact he encourages it, and he gives her piggybacks when she's tired.

He said something weird last time we were all out together in the park. He was pushing her on the swing and she was laughing her head off and shouting, 'Higher! Higher!' and I was sitting on the bench thinking, you lazy lump, Izzy, you can do that yourself if you want to.

After a while he came back exhausted and slumped on the bench beside me and I rubbed his hair and said, 'You'll make a great dad one day,' and he looked dead pleased and said, 'Are you proposing?' and I turned bright pink and spluttered, 'No!'

'Because if you are,' he continued, 'I'd say yes.' And the thing is, he wasn't joking, I could tell, because his eyes were dead serious and he gently tucked a stray strand of hair behind my ear. But then Izzy yelled, 'Je-em! Come and push me!' and he smiled ruefully, pressed his fingers to my lips and got up to do as he was told.

And I'm left thinking, did I imagine that? But I didn't because my heart was thudding nineteen to the dozen.

Mum's noticed what he's like. 'He's devoted to you!' she says and looks at me thoughtfully as if she's considering whether it's time for the big mother/ daughter chat, so I quickly make myself scarce.

She's right though, he never leaves me alone. If we're not together he rings me all the time on my mobile. He's given me his old one. It turned up after all this time; who would have thought it?

'A thief with a conscience,' he says one day. 'I found it in my school bag when I got home last night. Someone must have slipped it in yesterday. Pity they didn't return it before I bought my new one.'

'Do you reckon it was Darren?' I ask. 'I bet he's capable of something like that.'

'Could be,' he says, turning it over and examining it. 'Or Matt, maybe. Could be anyone. Anyway, you might as well have it. We can keep in touch better.'

'Shouldn't you let the school know it's turned up?'

He considers a minute, then says, 'Nah. No point in resurrecting all that stuff. Wouldn't be very nice for Mrs Walker, would it?'

See how he's changed? He's keeping his head down at school and staying out of trouble too. Like Megan said, I'm good for him.

'Come on, Izzie, you'll be late for school!'

It's Tuesday morning and Mum's had to go into work early so I've got to drop Izzy off on my way to school. She's been in the bathroom for ages. I hammer on the door.

'Izzy! Get a move on, will you?'

There's no reply. I push the door but it's bolted. She never locks it! (To be honest she usually sits resplendent on the loo with the door wide open on full display, like the Queen on her throne or an umpire at a tennis match. I'm always telling her off about it.) I put my ear to the door. From inside I can hear a snuffling sound.

'Izzy? Are you all right? Open the door.'

The bolt is drawn back and the handle turns and my little sister is revealed, a very woeful, quivering-chin, sorry-for-herself Iz, clutching her stomach.

'My tummy hurts!' she whines. 'I've got Appendicitis.'

No simple stomachache for this medical know-all. My heart sinks. I'm going to be late. The Dag will not be happy.

Neither will Jem. He'll be worried if I'm not on the bus.

'Come on, Iz. It'll have gone by the time you get to school.'

'It's going to burst!' she wails. 'Then I'll die!'

'No you won't.' I feel her forehead. It's nice and cool. 'Let me see your tongue.' She sticks it out obediently. It's a healthy pink to match her cheeks.

She's trying to pull a fast one, I know she is. I've just seen her wolf down a bowl of cereal and two pieces of toast with strawberry jam for breakfast and sneak a Jaffa Cake out of the cupboard when Mum wasn't looking.

'Come on. School,' I say firmly. Izzy collapses on the floor, holding her tummy and moaning, but I yank her upright and say sternly, 'OK, Izzy, what is it? What's wrong?'

She sniffs and draws her knees up to her chin, wrapping her arms around them. I sigh and sit down next to her, my back against the bathroom door, resigning myself to being late for school. Again. At last she says in a quiet, sad little voice, 'We've got a horrible new teacher.'

'Have you?' I sit up straight. 'What's happened to Miss Baker?'

'She's left.'

'Since when?'

She looks nonplussed. She has no conception of time.

'Was she in school yesterday?'

She shakes her head crossly. 'No! I told you, Kally, she's gone. We've got a new one now and I don't like her, she shouts all the time.'

Left! Laura Baker's left! An image jumps into my mind of two figures laughing together at a café table and for some odd reason I feel a sudden elation, until I catch sight of my little sister's woebegone face and reason reasserts itself.

'She's probably just sick, Iz. Teachers are off sick all the time then they come back when they're better.'

'Maybe she's got Appendicitis?' she says hopefully. 'Or what was that thing you said she had before? Stress? Do you think she's got Stress?'

'I expect so.' I think of the last time I saw her and remember how nervous she was. It wouldn't surprise me in the least. 'Anyway, I thought you didn't like her any more.'

Her eyes open wide in surprise. I'd forgotten about Izzy's famous selective memory. 'I love her, Kally,' she declares reverently. 'More than anyone else in the world.'

Oh. Thanks for that, Iz. 'Come on then. Let's go

and see if she's come back. She'll be wondering where you are.'

Izzy jumps up, tummyache forgotten. As we go out of the front door, suddenly she flings her arms around my waist and buries her face in my belly. 'I love you too, Kally,' she says indistinctly, her voice smothered in my school skirt. I press her close for a second and she peers up at me, her eyes brimming with affection. Aah, it's nice to have a little sister who thinks you're wonderful.

'Who do you love best?' I ask, savouring the moment. Izzie stares up at me, brow furrowed in concentration, nose and mouth moving from side to side as she considers. Silly question. I wish I hadn't asked. At last she comes to a decision.

'I know!' She smiles at me angelically. I squeeze her tight.

'Jem!' she announces, then disengages herself and runs ahead. 'Hurry up, Kally, we're going to be late!'

I bang the door behind me, grinning in spite of myself. Serves me right for asking.

Jem's texting me by the time I drop Izzy off. I don't wait to see if Miss Baker, Best Teacher Ever, is in, I just push her into the playground in the direction of Molly Moulton and say, 'Have fun!' before beating a hasty retreat.

`Where are you?` he asks.

`On my way!` I reply and then decide to leg it rather than wait for the next bus. Sometimes it gets on my nerves the way I have to account for my every move to Jem, though I wouldn't let him know that, he'd get upset. I mean it's flattering but it's a bit . . . I don't know, claustrophobic, I suppose. Anyway, I haven't got time to think about it now, I've got to get to school before the bell goes.

I make it by the skin of my teeth. The Dag looks daggers (well, she would, wouldn't she?) as I rush in but she hasn't got to my name yet on the register so I get away with it, just.

It's weird, have you noticed, sometimes when you start a day off in a rush, it seems to get worse as you go along, as if it builds up a momentum of its own and propels itself along at a crazy pace? You never really catch up with yourself. Well this turns out to be one of those days.

Double Science overruns and we miss break because we have to write up our experiment; at lunchtime we have to go to a meeting about next year's GCSE options and we end up gobbling down our sandwiches during afternoon registration to the Dag's annoyance and she makes us go back to the classroom at the end of school to clear up non-existent crumbs. I mean, what do they have cleaners for? I'm tempted not to go but I know it'll only mean trouble.

So it's way past the end of school when we finally get out.

'Will you be late for Izzy?' asks Megan.

'No, Mum's meeting her today; she's worked an early shift.'

Megan hesitates. 'Fancy a catch-up?'

'Yeah. Cool.' I smile at Megan in delight and she grins back. It's ages since we've spent time together on our own. She tucks her arm through mine and we fall into step and head towards town. Soon we're deep in conversation about a TV reality show that was on the night before, giggling our heads off at some of the antics the C-grade celebrities had got up to in the hope of reigniting the charred embers of their failing careers. So it's not till Jem suddenly swoops in front of us on his skateboard and bars our path that I actually give him a thought.

'Hiya!' I say, jumping back in surprise. 'Where did you spring from?'

'Where've you been all day?' He ignores my question.

'School.'

'Why aren't you collecting Izzy?'

'Mum is today. Change of plan.'

He circles us, his face impassive, just his jaw moving as he chews gum. Megan disengages herself from my arm and he weaves between and behind us.

'Where you going?'

'Town. Coming?'

He says nothing, just continues skating in a figure of eight, separating us with his wide, sweeping movements. It's quite spooky, mesmerizing if you know what I mean, in and out, in and out, silent except for the swish of the wheels.

'Actually,' says Megan, looking at her watch. 'Is that the time? Gosh. I think I'd better get straight home after all.'

'Gosh,' says Jem mockingly. 'Good idea. You wouldn't want Daddy worrying about you, would you?'

She gives him a filthy look and I say, 'No, don't! Megan?' but it's too late, she's off down the street, at a cracking pace, her blonde hair bouncing behind her. We watch her disappear round the corner. I sigh with disappointment.

'What did you say that for?'

'She changed her mind! Nothing to do with me. That's blondes for you. So unreliable.'

'You made her feel in the way.'

'She *was* in the way. Never mind,' says Jem, putting his arm around my shoulders, 'I'll give you a go on my skateboard if you're a good girl.'

I don't *want* a go on his skateboard! I want to catch up with Megan.

Then I feel mean. Poor Jem. It turns out he's been trying to find me all day. When I checked my phone I had dozens of messages on there from him, but I'd had it switched off in school of course.

Do you know what he did this morning? He'd got off the bus when he saw I wasn't on it and waited for the next one. I wasn't on that either because I'd decided to leg it. He made himself late for school, you know, and got a detention, all because of me.

He wasn't mad at me though.

'Just let me know exactly what you're doing next time,' was all he said. He's really learning to control his feelings.

I'm so lucky. Some boys just use their girlfriends to show off to their mates, but me, I'm the centre of Jem's existence.

But it *would* have been nice to go to town with Megan.

I feel *really* bad now. Jem, who's been soooo good lately, keeping his nose clean at school, is in trouble again and it's ALL MY FAULT.

In the end he threw a strop about the detention. He tried to explain reasonably to Mr Davey that he'd been in plenty of time but then had been concerned about me so had ended up being late through no fault of his own, but the Assistant Head was having none of it.

'It's your responsibility to be at school on time and nobody else's,' he says shortly. I've gone along with Jem for support but it's useless. Mr Davey waves us aside like we're two annoying, persistent bluebottles that he'd like to swat with a newspaper. 'You're not glued at the hip, you know.'

'I was worried about Kally, Sir.' Jem ignores the jibe and speaks quietly and politely. I'm proud of him. There's no trace of the tough-talking, confrontational, old Jem.

Mr Davey has got to be impressed by the new one.

Or not. 'You don't need to hold your girlfriend's hand to get to school on time, Jermaine. And you don't need her here to plead your case, either. You're a big boy now. It's about time you stood on your own two feet.'

I gasp. Put-down or what? Why was Mr Davey being so horrible? Suddenly I think of Megan disappearing last night when Jem arrived. I bet she's been complaining to her dad about Jem and me.

'Come on, Jem, it's useless,' I say and turn to go. Not Jem. He's as still as a statue, his face drained of colour. He *hates* being made to look stupid.

The tension in the room is palpable, as if we all know a bomb is about to go off and there's nothing anyone can do to stop it. My heart sinks. He's worked it out too.

I tug Jem by the arm. 'Jem! Let's go!' He shakes me off. His lips twist into his famous sardonic smile.

'Been running home to Daddy with her tales, has she? Aah, Diddums. Well, you can tell her from me, she can't hide behind her daddy all her life.'

'Jermaine, I'm warning you!' Mr Davey looks as if he's about to grab hold of Jem and slam him against the wall.

'Go on then, hit me!' taunts Jem, jutting his jaw into the teacher's face and pointing at it. 'Hit me!'

'Jem! Stop it!' I yell. 'Stop it now!'

The sound of my voice has more effect on Mr Davey

than Jem. He stands rigid, glaring at Jem. I can see a pulse beating in his forehead, then he rubs his hand over his mouth and chin and takes a deep breath.

'Jermaine Smith, I am suspending you from this school for a period of five days. You will remain in the school office until your parent or guardian comes to collect you. You are dismissed.'

He sounds so formal, like a policeman placing a criminal under arrest. I say, 'Come on, Jem, let's go,' and put my hand on Jem's arm and this time he allows me to lead him out of the room. He's trembling with rage. At the door he turns back and scowls at Mr Davey.

'This isn't over yet,' he says. His voice is quiet now, he's under control again, but for some reason this freaks me out even more.

I'm in the new block doing Science when I see Jem going home. It's got big, plate-glass windows and you get a good view of the main entrance. I watch as he swaggers down the steps and crosses the yard as if he hasn't got a care in the world. An overweight woman, with untidy greying hair, wearing a coat of unfashionable length and indeterminate colour, scuttles behind him. Jem's mum. Somehow I hadn't imagined her like that. Behind them, Mr Davey stands by the main door with his arms folded, as if he's escorting them off the premises. I turn around and catch Megan watching them too. She colours and bends her head over her work.

When school's over, I'm collecting my stuff from my locker when she appears beside me. 'We need to talk.'

'Do we?' I thrust my homework in my bag and haul it on to my shoulder before I glance at her coolly. Her eyes are pleading.

'I didn't mean for any of this to happen, you know.'

'Really?' I turn away.

'Kally, listen to me. There's something you should know.'

'What?'

'It's about Jem . . .'

This time I walk away, but she still doesn't get the message. Outside she catches up with me and puts her hand on my arm. 'Kally, listen! It's something my father told me . . .'

Across the road I can see Jem waiting for me. He's leaning back against the railings by the bus stop but he stands up straight when he spots me talking to Megan and for a moment he looks anxious, as if he's not sure of me. Oh Jem! You can trust me more than that. I shake off Megan's hand and snap, 'You shouldn't believe all you hear! Believe me, people can get things very wrong and that's something I've learnt from *my* father.'

'Kally, wait!' she says but it's too late, I've run across the road into Jem's arms. By the time we've emerged from our kiss, she's nowhere to be seen and we stand around chatting for a while with Darren and those who want to know what's going on, before we start to make our way home, arms round each other. Then all of a sudden a car pulls up next to us and Mr Davey winds the window down. On the back seat I can see Megan, head down, her face strained and unhappy.

'Your suspension includes the surrounding area of the school as well, Jermaine. Don't let me see you hanging around again or I'll make it my business to make sure your exclusion will be permanent.'

I can feel Jem tensing. Before he explodes, I pipe up indignantly, 'You can't do that, Sir. That's victimization, that is.'

'Just watch me,' he snaps. 'And by the way, Kally, tomorrow I want to see your mother too.'

I gasp as he pulls out into the road. That's all I need.

'He's asking for it,' says Jem with a cold gleam in his eyes and takes a run and kick at a discarded can lying on the road. It soars into the air and bounces off the back of the car with a clatter. For a moment I'm terrified Mr Davey is going to stop the car and get out and give Jem what for but the car is caught in the stream of traffic and has to move on. 'And he's going to get it,' adds Jem, under his breath, and pulls me back into the shelter of his arm.

⋆ ⋆ ⋆

'What's it about?' asks Mum, looking surprised, when I break the news her presence is requested by the Assistant Head.

'Jem got a detention for being late because he waited for me,' I explain, making a conscious decision to keep detail to the minimum. 'He complained and Mr Davey lost it and suspended him from school.'

'That doesn't sound very fair,' says Mum, frowning. Not surprisingly, like me, she has a heightened sense of injustice. 'But I still don't see what this has to do with me.'

I decide it's the time for honesty. 'He's probably going to tell you Jem's a bad influence on me.'

'Why?'

'Because he gets into trouble at school, Mum.'

She looks worried. 'He seems such a *nice* boy . . .'

'He is. *You* know what it's like . . . Once you get labelled as a villain you've got no chance.'

Her lips tighten. We've tuned into the same wavelength. 'As far as I'm concerned, Jem is a thoughtful, helpful, considerate boy and I shall tell Mr Davey so tomorrow.' I breathe a sigh of relief.

Three reasons.

1. Mum's on our side.
2. She couldn't have been bothered to be on anyone's

side a few months ago. She's definitely on the mend.

3. She's not going to stop me seeing Jem.

The next day when I come out of school I relay this conversation to Jem. By phone, of course, since STC and its surrounding area is a Total Exclusion Zone to him.

'Your mum's ace,' he says.

'What's yours like, Jem?'

There's a silence at the other end. Jem always clams up if his mother's mentioned, I've noticed, and I'm beginning to wonder what the mystery is. I know she hasn't got two heads now I've actually seen her at last. She looked perfectly normal to me, disappointingly so in fact. I'd expected someone a bit more exotic to be the mother of Jem.

'Come round and see,' he says casually.

'What, now?'

'Why not? You know where I live, don't you?'

'Yep. Be there in ten.'

I snap my phone shut, shaking with excitement. He wants me to meet his mum! Jem's never so much as invited me to his house before. He's so private, he's never even told me his address. Oh no! I suddenly realized, he'll be wondering how I know it! (One day I had a sly look in the form register, the hard copy they keep in the office, while I was waiting for someone to bandage my knee after a fall in netball, if you must know.) He'll think I'm a stalker!

I'm there in eight.

Salubrious Place is not like it sounds. It's a row of small, identical houses, straight on the street, with few distinguishing features. When I draw near, Number 15 has a heavy beat of music pulsating from the top window. In all other respects it is like all the others: front door painted a restrained shade of blue; neat curtains veiling the window; a large pot containing a plant with fleshy green leaves which screens the dark room beyond from any eyes intent on prying.

Mine included! I press my face against the window but all I can make out is the dim outline of a table and chairs. It looks so boring! I can't believe Jem lives here! I catch a movement at the back of the room and jump back but it's too late, the front door opens and a voice barks, 'What do you want?'

My cheeks flame with embarrassment as I realize I've been copped and I say apologetically, 'Mrs Smith?' because it's the woman I saw following Jem out of school, only this time she's wearing an overall and has curlers in her hair. Close up I can see she's older than I thought, with wrinkles, and pouches round her eyes, and furrowed worry lines running from her nose to her cheeks. Her eyes narrow.

'Do I know you?'

'I'm here to see Jem.'

'He's grounded. Been in trouble at school.'

'I know. I'm Kally.'

'Kally?' She studies me and frowns. My stomach sinks into my shoes. She's going to tell me to get lost. But then a door opens somewhere upstairs releasing a blast of heavy rock music and Jem appears at the top of the stairs.

'Kally? Is that you?'

I cough with embarrassment. 'Yes.' My voice sounds high and squeaky.

'Well send her up then!' yells Jem, his voice impatient and cross.

Mrs Smith holds the door open a fraction wider. 'First on the right,' she sniffs. I press past her in the small hallway and gallop up the stairs as fast as possible.

Jem is standing in front of a door with 'KEEP OUT!' painted on it in thick, black capitals, looking amused. 'Found it then? I couldn't remember if you knew my address.' I can feel myself blushing.

'Turn that noise down,' yells his mum up the stairs. Jem scowls down at her then deliberately slams the door shut.

'Jem! That's no way to treat your mother!' I say reproachfully, sinking on to his bed and looking around. My heart misses a beat.

Jem's walls are covered from top to bottom with pictures of me. Me skating, concentrating; me on the beach, laughing, my hair whipped across my face; me on the school field chatting animatedly, though no sign of the person I'm talking to; me with my eyes closed, lying in the sun. There's an odd one or two of Izzy as well, but basically his room is a shrine to me. I gulp. In Ancient Rome they called such a room a Nymphaeum. We did it in history.

I had no idea he'd taken so many photos of me. I laugh nervously.

'No wonder your mum looked as if she recognized me.'

This time he scowls at me.

'That's not my mum. Give me a break.'

I'm late home and I wonder if I'm going to be in for it from Mum. Plus I've remembered she's been into school today to see Mr Davey and now I'm anxious to find out what he's said to her. But when we turn into our lane I can see her on the doorstep talking to some couple. It's Geoff and a woman I presume is Pat. They all turn to look at us.

'Walked you home, has he?' says Geoff, stating the obvious. 'Good to see some lads still have a sense of responsibility.' He smiles benevolently at Jem from behind his bushy white beard. Izzy, no longer in awe of Geoff, is hanging from his arm but when she spots Jem, my fickle little sister disentangles herself.

'Come and watch telly with me!' she exclaims in delight, flinging her arms round him, but Mum shakes her head.

'It's nearly time for bed, madam. School tomorrow.'

'I'd better be off home,' says Jem. 'See you, Kally. Bye, Mrs O'Connor.'

'Bye.'

'Seems like a nice lad,' says Pat. She's round with brown hair sprinkled with grey, like salt and pepper mixed together, and smiley eyes. They can't be real, these two. Mrs Pepperpot, married to Father Christmas. Mum doesn't answer. Is it my imagination or is she being a bit distant towards Jem?

'He is,' I say and wave him goodbye as he turns the corner. 'What's for tea, Mum?'

'Tea? You should come home on time if you want some tea!' says Mum, but her tone is playful. I study her warily. Actually, she doesn't look cross. There's a kind of light-heartedness about her.

Pat beams at me. 'Always hungry at that age, aren't they? Come on, Geoff, let's be off. Jan's got things to do.'

'Thanks for everything,' says Mum and gives her a hug, then she embraces Geoff too as if they're both long-lost friends. Weird.

Even more weird, Geoff grabs her by the arms and stares into her eyes meaningfully. 'Like I said, it can only be a matter of time now, all being well,' he says.

'We'll see,' answers Mum, but she looks happier than I've seen her for ages. What's going on?

'What's all that about?' I ask, as soon as she closes the door.

'Oh, just stuff about the shop,' she says vaguely and goes off into the kitchen to organize some food. I wander into the sitting room where Izzy's already plugged into her evening's viewing. She's curled up on the sofa engrossed in *Holby City*. I'm bursting to talk to someone and all I've got is a hypochondriac six-year-old for company.

'How's Miss Baker?' I ask politely.

'Sshh.'

'Is she back?'

'Back where?'

'In school, idiot.'

'Look!' She points with excitement at the television. The surgeon has just sliced into a large piece of human flesh while flirting with his registrar and arguing with his anaesthetist. Blood spurts out impressively. 'He's removing a blood clot! He's doing a Thrombo, Thrombi, Thrombectomy!' she says triumphantly. She's amazing. I wouldn't have a clue, but she's like a sponge when it comes to medical matters, she soaks them up. I sit next to her and we spend a silent but satisfying hour, me engrossed in the tangled relationships of the staff of the Holby hospital, Izzy enthralled by the complex surgical technicalities, fortified by plates of beans on toast that Mum brings in from the kitchen.

As soon as the theme tune plays at the end, Mum says firmly, 'Bed, young lady,' and I know for sure when she comes back downstairs from putting Izzy to bed, I'm going to be in for the third degree. I'm not wrong.

'I saw Mr Davey today,' she says, with ginormous lack of subtlety, sitting down in the chair opposite. I grunt, pretending I'm engrossed in the programme on the television. 'Turn that off, Kally, I want to speak to you.'

I do as I'm told, clicking my tongue for appearance's sake, though in actual fact I'm dying to find out what tales Mr Davey's been spinning. Mum looks serious but not in an Oh-no-my-daughter-needs-an-asbo-what-am-I-going-to-do-with-her? way so I relax a bit. There's something different about her tonight, there's an energy about her. She's like a saucepan simmering on the stove, full to the brim with emotion, with the lid tightly jammed on so it doesn't bubble over. What's going on inside? Agitation? Distress? I don't think so. It's more like anticipation or hope or something. Excitement, that's what it is.

What's she got to be excited about? More hours at the shop, probably. Yippee.

'He's worried about the effect Jem's having on you.'

I sigh. 'I told you so.'

'He's afraid he'll lead you astray.'

'What?' I'm justifiably aggrieved. 'Astray as in getting my homework in on time? Astray as in doing well in my exams? Astray as in improving my skating technique. Yeah, Mum, he's right. Jem's a really bad influence on me.'

Mum chuckles in spite of herself. 'Sarky! Mind you, that's what *I* said, more or less.'

'Did you?'

'Yes. I told him Jem's been a great help to us and how devoted he is to you.'

Good old Mum. 'What did he say?'

'Something odd.' Mum looks thoughtful. 'He said that's what he's concerned about. He thinks Jem's too fond of you and the problem will be when you've had enough.'

I stiffen. I can hear Jem's voice, sobbing.

Don't leave me, Kally. You won't leave me, will you?

'What's he mean by that?'

Mum shakes her head. 'Search me. I asked him that very question but he went all tight-lipped on me and said he wasn't at liberty to elaborate.'

You'll get fed up with me soon like everyone else.

I stir uneasily. 'What's it got to do with him anyway?'

'Not a lot. Some of these teachers think they're social workers nowadays.' Her mouth purses. It's not so long ago since she was asked to keep me at home from my old school till all the fuss died down. She was furious at the time.

'Anyway,' I grumble, 'the problem's hypothetical because I'm not planning to dump Jem. Why would I? We get on great, you know that.'

Mum nods. 'Well, just be careful, Kally. And let me know if there are any problems. You know I'm here to help.'

Is that it? Is that the end of this conversation? Apparently so. For a moment I'm tempted to say, 'Mum? To be honest Jem does act weird sometimes. I don't quite know what to do.'

But she's leafing through the TV pages of the paper and she cries, 'Look what's on! Why didn't you remind me! It's the final part of that drama we were watching last week. Switch the telly back on, Kal.'

We settle down to watch the programme together. It's a thriller, a good one, the last of a three-parter, and all the strands of the story are coming together in this final episode. I've been looking forward to it. Only I can't concentrate because my own private drama is unfolding in my head.

All those photos! There's too many. It's freaky.

Everyone leaves me in the end.

Next to me, Mum's not following it either; for all her enthusiasm, her mind's elsewhere. She's got a pen in her hand and she's doodling away on the back of an envelope. I glance at it. It's quite good actually, like one of those pop art pictures from the sixties, a psychedelic mixture of scribbles, patterns, flowers and horses' heads. Freud would have something to say about that! I look closer. I can see now she's woven *Steve O'Connor* over and over again in bubble writing into her artistic masterpiece.

'When's he coming out, Mum?'

Startled, her head jerks up.

'What?'

'When are we going to see Dad again?'

Mum bites her lip. I shouldn't have asked. Then she says so quietly I have to strain to hear, 'Soon, Kally love. Soon I hope.'

'Really?' I sit bolt upright. 'What's happened?'

Mum inhales deeply and holds it as if she's considering something so important she daren't even breathe. At last she lets out a huge sigh. 'I don't really want to discuss it with you because I don't want to raise your hopes. But it looks as if some new evidence has come to light. There may be an appeal.'

'You mean he'll be freed?' I'm overjoyed. 'Mum, that's fantastic!' I fling myself at her and hug her so tight it hurts. 'He *told* them he didn't do anything wrong. Why didn't they listen?'

Mum pats me on the back and sits back. Her eyes are

concerned. 'Kally, you mustn't get too excited. Nothing's going to happen overnight.'

'Why not? If they know he's not guilty, they can't keep him in jail!'

'It's not as simple as that. They need to re-examine the evidence of a key witness but she's gone missing.'

'Who?' But I know the answer even as I ask the question. '*She's* gone missing.' It could only be one person.

Emma Preston.

Mum won't talk about it any more. 'I've said too much already. And don't you say a word about this to anyone, Kally. It could jeopardize the outcome.'

'Mum! I've never said a thing!' I protest.

'I know,' she says and hugs me again. 'Now bed!'

My head's reeling. Upstairs Izzy is sprawled on my side of the bed. I nudge her over.

'She's not back yet,' she mumbles sleepily.

'Who?'

'Miss Baker. It's not fair, I love her,' but she lapses back into sleep. My phone displays a message from Jem. I open it guiltily. Jem's vanished clean out of my head after Mum's exciting news.

`Thanks for listening. Luv u.`

I text back. `Luv u 2. I'm going to sleep now.`

`Sweet dreams`, he replies.

Huh! Wishful thinking! I've got so much stuff jumbled up in my head there's no room for dreams. I wish I could take it all out, give it a good shake and get it sorted into some kind of order.

Or I wish I could take some of it to a charity shop and dispose of it permanently. Give it to some other poor soul to worry about.

Though I wouldn't wish a dad in prison for something he didn't do on anyone.

And a boyfriend with issues, that's quite hard too.

Now I know why Jem can be so difficult at times. It's not his fault at all.

It's his mum's.

I don't quite know how to say this without me sounding really really mean. Perhaps it's not mean if you're just admitting it to yourself. It would be different if I said it to Megan or Holly or the rest of the girls.

The thing is, this week that Jem's suspended from school, it's OK. It's fine. It's good, actually.

I'm enjoying school more without him.

There. I knew I would sound horrible. But it's true.

I thought it would be strange. He's always there, you see. On the bus, morning break, lunchtime, after school, he's always waiting there, waiting for me. Once Mr Davey had warned him off though, he had to keep his distance, not just during the school day, obviously, but before and after it too. Yesterday I resigned myself to being a Billy-No-Mates for a week but today when I get on the bus, Holly calls me up to the back.

'Come and sit here with us!' she says. 'Don't sit down there on your own.'

You know, Holly's not so bad when you get to know her. I mean, after what Jem did to her I wouldn't blame her if she never spoke to me again, but here she was making sure I didn't feel lonely. She never split on him either. I sit down next to her and she offers me a fag. I shake my head and she shrugs. 'Suit yourself,' she says and blows a smoke ring. 'See what you're missing?' Then she chokes and splutters and everyone laughs and Darren thumps her on the back.

It suddenly occurs to me that, daft as she is, everyone likes Holly. Well, most people do. Jem certainly doesn't. Mind you, he doesn't like anyone at STC.

Except me.

I thought it would be really awkward with Megan. I had no intention of speaking to her because, of course, I blame her for Jem getting suspended, and yesterday, I didn't. I maintained a dignified silence all day and everyone respected it which was satisfying but incredibly boring and lonely.

But then today I walk in the classroom with Holly and we're in the middle of a conversation about that programme last night, because, of course, I missed it and, before we know it, everyone else is joining in including Megan. By the time the bell goes and the Dag walks in, it's as if nothing's ever happened. At break and lunchtime we sit around and chat again and have a laugh and no one mentions Jem.

After school I'm feeling a bit guilty about Jem so I go round to see him. I can hear the music as I walk down the street. This time I ring the bell but when she opens the door, Mrs Smith still glares at me.

'He's grounded, you know. He's not supposed to see anyone,' she says, but then Jem appears behind her and kind of pushes her aside and says, 'Come on in, Kal, ignore her,' and I don't know what to do, so in the end I smile apologetically at her and do as he says as if I haven't got a mind of my own.

'Poor thing,' he says, giving me a kiss as soon as he's closed the door of his bedroom. 'It must be so boring at school all day with nobody with even half a brain to talk to.'

'It's not so bad,' I say truthfully. His face falls. 'I miss you though,' I add hastily. I'm feeling a bit weird actually. The thing is, I'm surrounded by images of me and it's pretty spooky.

And I hate the way he speaks to his mum.

Only she's not his mum.

She's his grandmother.

His real mother doesn't live with him. He told me all about it the other night. Now he's talking about her again. Having kept it all to himself for ages it's as if he's pulled the plug and all this stuff is gushing out about her.

'She's young. Too young. She wasn't much more than a kid herself when she had me. She's never really known what to do with me.'

'Where is she?'

'Up London way I think.' He shrugs. 'To be honest I haven't got a clue. I haven't heard from her for ages.' He looks so sad. My heart aches for him.

'What's she like?'

'Slim. Blonde. Good-looking . . .'

That's blondes for you. So unreliable.

I try to lighten the mood. 'Take after your dad then, do you?'

'What?'

'Good-looking?'

'Cheek!' He considers. 'Yeah, suppose I do. I'm dark like him, that's for sure. He was a singer in a band. He pushed off back to America when I was a baby so I don't really know if I look like him or not.' His mouth twists into a bitter smile. 'Like I said, Kally, everyone leaves me sooner or later.'

I could cry for him. My hand steals into his and grasps it tight.

'Have you always lived with your gran?'

'Nope. I've lived with my mum on and off. It's great

for a bit, then she meets someone new and wants to move on so she ditches me. I've lived with all sorts of people over the years, anyone she can dump me on.'

'Jem! I had no idea.'

'Anyway, that's why I'm living with Gran at the moment. She doesn't want me here either.'

I'm outraged. 'You shouldn't be treated like that!'

He sighs. 'You get used to it. I'm a big boy now.'

He's lying. You don't get used to being rejected like that, how could you? You just build a protective shell around yourself and make out to the world you're a hard man. But inside you're just an abandoned child looking for someone to love you.

It explains such a lot.

Impulsively, I fling my arms around his neck and hug him.

Then I open my eyes and see his bedroom walls plastered with pictures of me and a tiny trickle of fear seeps into my consciousness.

He thinks Jem's too fond of you. The problem will be when you've had enough.

Mr Davey knows about Jem's background, doesn't he? He's got files on us all.

'I'm so lucky to have found you, Kally,' Jem whispers.

'Me too,' I say.

But to be honest I'm dead uncomfortable with it all. I

feel trapped. Like how could I ever walk away from Jem knowing how he's already been rejected by that evil mother of his? I don't want to, don't get me wrong. But I couldn't, even if I did. This is HEAVY, HEAVY, HEAVY.

So after a while I make an excuse and go home.

Maybe that's why I'm enjoying school this week without him. A bit of freedom to be me, to have a laugh with everyone without worrying about upsetting Jem. I know I sound like a callous cow, I know I sound as if *I'm* rejecting Jem now, but it's only for a little while. Like a holiday from Jem.

So I make the most of it. After school I go down town and do girly things with Megan and Holly. We drink smoothies, trying each other's concoctions ('Kiwi and beetroot! I don't think so, Holly!'); we rifle through the magazines in the stationer's, competing for the most hair-raising stories (I win with 'Crash-dieting made me turn into a knife-wielding werewolf!') until the manager tells us to clear off if we have no intention of buying; we try on the most outrageously funky outfits and fall apart at our hideous style crimes. I haven't had so much fun since Ella.

We're in the chemist's sampling the lip-gloss and slapping on the bronzer ('Not with your colouring, darling!') when I'm suddenly aware of being the object of someone's attention. I catch a glimpse of a girl disappearing into the next aisle and my heart misses a beat. Without saying anything to the others I slip after her.

'Miss Baker? Laura?'

She turns around and smiles tentatively at me. 'Hello, Kally.'

'How are you?'

She moves her shoulders. 'Oh, you know . . .'

'Izzy misses you.'

'I miss her too. I miss them all.' She looks upset.

'Will you be back soon?'

'No.' She hesitates. 'I'm moving away.'

'You're not! Don't you like it here? I didn't either when I first came but now I've settled in.' It's true. I hadn't realized it till now.

'Oh the place is all right. And I love my job. But . . . well, actually, I've had a bit of trouble since I've been here.'

'What sort of trouble?'

She seems reluctant, as if she's said too much already. 'I don't really want to go into it.'

I feel myself colouring up. 'I'm sorry, it's none of my business. I don't mean to pry.'

'No, it's all right.' She puts out a hand and touches me. 'It's kind of you to ask. The thing is, I don't want to resurrect it all. It's over now, but it was scary at the time.'

My blood chills. I remember what she was like that last day I picked Izzy up from her class. I knew it! She was frightened of someone.

'Did you tell anyone? Your head teacher? The police?'

She shakes her head, looking as if she's about to cry.

'Why not?' I don't need to know all this, but I can't resist probing further. It's like she's a sore tooth and I can't stop prodding her even though I know I'll feel another jab of pain.

'What could they do? It was just something that got out of hand. It was probably my fault in the first place, I must have encouraged hi— it without realizing. Anyway, like I said,' she takes a deep breath and looks at me squarely for the first time, 'it's all over and done with now.'

'Is it? Then don't go! Izzy will be gutted if you do!'

'Oh, Izzy will be fine. She's tougher than you think.' She smiles weakly.

'Where are you going?'

She hesitates. 'I'd rather not say.'

Icicles start to form around my heart.

'Kally?' Megan appears behind me. 'You coming?'

'I've got to go,' I say. 'All the best, anyway.'

'Thanks,' she says and then she totally takes me by surprise because she puts her arms round me and gives me a quick hug.

'Take care, Kally,' she whispers in my ear then she

walks away fast, looking as gorgeous from the back view as she does from the front with a figure you would die for and blonde hair waxed into peaks.

'Who's that?' asks Megan curiously.

A solid block of ice has lodged itself into the middle of my chest.

'Kally! Talk to me! Are you all right?'

Megan swims back into focus, her eyes full of concern. I shiver.

'She's nobody,' I say. 'Nobody important.'

At the weekend I stay close to home. When Jem rings to go skating on Saturday, unbelievably I make an excuse.

'There's stuff going on with Dad. Mum needs me around at the moment.'

'I need you too, Kally.'

'Mum needs me more.'

There's a a pause. Then Jem says, 'You never told me what the big mystery is with your dad.'

'There *is* no big mystery!' I snap but when he falls silent I feel rotten. I want to spend time with Mum, what with the appeal and everything, but I know Jem wants to be with me too, especially as we've hardly seen each other this week. But the honest truth is, I'm not sure I want to be with him, not at the moment.

'Don't you want to be with me, Kally?'

'Of course I do!' What is he, a mind-reader?

'It's just that, ever since I told you about my mum,

we've hardly seen each other. I knew I shouldn't have said anything.' He sounds gutted. 'Now you're fed up with me too.'

'No! Absolutely not!'

But I am. A bit.

The trouble is, it's always so complicated with Jem.

My week of freedom has spoilt me, shown me what it's like to be a normal fourteen-year-old, doing normal teenage stuff. No angst about Rejection and Abandonment and Anger Management and all those other problems you're only supposed to come across in Personal and Social Education lessons: just a giggle in school with the others with no strings attached. It's been a great week. Apart from the Laura Baker episode.

'You've got to admit this relationship is a bit one-sided,' he continues.

'How do you make that out?' I'm edgy, wrong-footed.

'Well, for instance, I've told you loads of things about me, stuff I've never told anyone else, like about my mum, but I know nothing about you. How d'you think that makes me feel?'

I'm silent.

'Kally, if you won't confide in me, you're saying you don't trust me. That's no basis for a relationship.'

'I know.' My voice is a whisper.

There's a pause.

‘Do you want to finish with me? Is that what you want?’ he asks.

‘No!’ What’s wrong with me? His level, reasoning voice brings me to my senses. He’s been honest and trusting enough to tell me all about his own personal baggage. The least I can do is to be as honest and open with him as he’s been with me.

‘Tell you what. Tomorrow we’ll skate. Then after that you can come back to mine and we’ll have a chat, yeah? I’ll tell you anything you want to know.’

‘Are you sure?’

‘Yep. You’re right. If I can’t trust you, who can I trust? The only thing is . . .’

‘What?’

‘You may not want to know me when you’ve heard what I’ve got to say.’

‘Kally,’ he says, ‘I will want to know you for the rest of my life.’

The next day we have a ball. Jem decides he’s bored with all our usual haunts and wants to try something new. He takes me to an industrial estate on the edge of town, deserted on a Sunday. ‘On the edge’ is right, this place is grim and desolate, like the film set of a violent B-movie. But we’re left to our own devices with no angry car owners telling us to clear off so we make the most of it.

There's something about Jem today, he's sparking. Me, I'm content to carve around for a bit, get the picture first before I attempt anything, but him, he's really up for it. He finds the highest rails he can and 50/50s along them, ollys over huge, high gaps that would break his neck if he fell into them, kick-flips over metal struts and even climbs up on to the roof of a three-storey building to taildrop on to the flat roof below. He is in serious death-defying mood and it rubs off on me and soon I'm attempting tricks I've never done before. When I nosegrind along a ledge for the first time, it's mind-blowing.

'That was brilliant!' I beam at Jem, my arm around his waist as we make our way back to my place. He looks gorgeous in white T-shirt and low-slung, baggy jeans, beanie pulled down over his ears. Vitality radiates from him even though he's been doing tricks non-stop for the past couple of hours. This is what I like about Jem, all that raw energy. He stops and bends his head and we kiss and I wonder how I could ever have thought I didn't want to be with him.

Back home, we have tea with Mum and Iz. It's interesting. Mum's been baking and Izzy's been in charge of fillings.

'Muffin?' offers Mum sweetly. 'Blueberry, chocolate or tomato sauce?'

'My idea,' explains Izzy unnecessarily, giving us a wide,

crimson-toothed smile. 'Blood Muffins!'

I accept one as the lesser of two evils. Jem bravely tucks into a fairy cake decorated with mayonnaise and a pickled onion. 'Eyeball cakes,' explains Izzy. 'Take two!'

Afterwards we escape upstairs while Mum listens to Izzy read. 'Maybe when she can follow a recipe she'll be a little more conventional in the culinary stakes,' calls Jem from the bathroom where he's depositing a napkinful of sticky, mayonnaisy mess down the loo.

'Izzy? Conventional? She's obsessed by bodies.'

'Me too,' says Jem, lying down beside me on my bed.

I wriggle away. 'Izzy'll be up soon.'

'Excuses.' He props himself up on his elbow, studying me, his head resting on his hand. 'We've had a good time today, haven't we, Kal?'

I smile. 'The best.'

He kisses me gently.

'Tell me about your dad.'

I stiffen. Mum's voice is in my ear.

Don't you say a word about this to anyone, Kally.

'Not now. We haven't got time. Izzy . . .'

'Will be up soon. I know, you said. So stop wasting time and get on with it.'

'I can't. I promised Mum I wouldn't.'

Jem considers my words. 'Then you shouldn't break a promise.'

I fall silent, thinking. She told Geoff, didn't she? He catches a curl that's escaped from my band and pulls it out tight. It springs back and he does it again. And again. It's strangely soothing.

I want to tell him, now he's no longer putting any pressure on me.

'I promised you as well though, didn't I? I said I'd tell you anything you wanted to know.'

'It's OK, Kally. I understand.'

He's so considerate, so . . . decent. Another person, someone like Holly for instance, would have kept on till they *made* me tell them.

'But I just want you to know, you can trust me, Kal. I'd never breathe a word to anyone.' His eyes are clear and candid.

He's devoted to you. That's what Mum said about him. She wouldn't mind me telling Jem, would she?

For goodness' sake, Kally, says my inner voice. This is Jem who thinks the world of you. This is what it's all about. Trust. What have you got to fear?

So I begin, hesitant at first, stumbling over my words, but as soon as I start to recall the order of events, the whole sorry tale comes pouring out, right from the beginning.

I tell him about my first board, a present from my parents, blue and covered in flowers, and how I immediately customized it with skulls and cross-bones, and he laughs and says, 'Good on you, girl!' I tell him about my dad raising money for the skate-park and he says, 'He sounds like a good bloke,' and listens appreciatively to the stuff we got up to. I tell him about Emma Preston and how the money disappeared and he falls silent, with a frown on his face.

But all the time, he pulls that curl out, slowly, hypnotically, to its full extent and lets it bounce back, and that keeps me going and I tell him my dad's in prison now, for a crime he didn't commit.

At the end I'm trembling. I've never told a soul before, not the whole story, just denied it hotly at my last school that my dad had done anything wrong, usually with my fists. Putting it into words like this makes it sound so serious. And the thing is, Jem doesn't know Dad, does he? He doesn't know he's incapable of pulling a stunt like that. I wish I hadn't said anything now. Mum told me not to!

I sob in panic. Jem pulls me to him and holds me. 'It's OK,' he says, stroking my hair, 'I've got you.' He rocks me gently and sings to me softly like I'm a baby in his arms, and gradually I quieten down and then I realize he's not singing, he's chanting, the same words, over and over again, like a mantra. After a while I ask, 'What are you saying?'

'The first line of a poem. It's called "This be the verse".'

'Say it out loud.'

'They fuck you up, your mum and dad . . .'

'Jem!' I sit up and look at him wide-eyed. 'You don't use swear words in poetry.'

'You can do whatever you like. Anyway, I didn't make it up, a guy called Philip Larkin did, donkeys' years ago. Poets reveal what's going on deep inside them so they're going to use strong language, it stands to reason.'

I'd never thought of it like that. 'I thought poetry was all about daffodils and highwaymen and romantic love.' We hardly did any at STC, certainly nothing as interesting as this. The Dag would slap me in detention and Philip Larkin with me if I said that line in class. 'D'you know the rest of it?'

'Just the first verse.

They fuck you up, your mum and dad
They may not mean to, but they do.
They fill you with the faults they had
And add some extra, just for you.'

Jem grins. 'Don't look so shocked. It's true, isn't it? Even all those years ago when this bloke was writing, parents were messing up their kids' lives for them.'

I stare at Jem with respect. He never ceases to surprise me. How many guys could quote Philip Larkin at you? I'd never even heard of the bloke. But I'm troubled.

'He didn't mean to though.'

'Who?'

'Dad. He didn't mean to, you know, mess up my life. He was trying to help.'

Jem laughs at the way I avoid using the word. 'That's what the poet says. He did though, didn't he? Like my mum did to me. We've got that in common, you and me. We've both been screwed up by our parents.'

I wriggle uncomfortably. 'I'm not . . . screwed up. I'm just sad because my dad's in jail and he shouldn't be. It's not like this poet geezer says. It's not Dad's fault.'

Jem pulls me close again. 'You're so loyal, Kally. That's what I love about you. You'll never let anyone down.'

I don't know about that. Why does he always put me on a pedestal?

Suddenly the door opens to reveal Izzy and we spring apart. For a moment I'm scared she's overheard us but she beams at us from ear to ear.

'I forgot you were still here, Jem. Is he sleeping with us tonight, Kally?'

Jem catches my eye and grins at me cheekily. 'Now there's an invitation. You'd better square it with your mother first.'

'NO!'

Too late. 'Mum!' yells Izzy down the stairs. 'Can Jem sleep with Kally tonight?'

I chuck my pillow at him. The next minute Mum's voice calls up. 'I don't know what's going on up there but it's time Jem went home!'

'Idiot!' I hiss but he's rolling about hooting with laughter. Izzy dives on top of him and he tickles her till she shrieks for mercy. In the end Mum appears and says, 'Jermaine Smith, what on earth are you doing to my daughters? Out!' but she's laughing.

Jem picks his beanie up off the floor and pulls it on, still chuckling. He looks drop-dead gorgeous when he's happy. As he passes Mum he salutes and she pretends to clip him round the ear so he ducks and she misses him and they both burst out laughing.

Why can't it always be like this?

Needless to say, Jem's not back at school two minutes before he's causing mayhem. It was inevitable. He was always going to get his own back on Megan and Mr Davey; they had become his enemies. If you're not for Jem, you're against him.

He makes Megan nervous now. She, who used to be Miss Super-Cool, goes out of her way to avoid him. Now I hardly see anything of her outside the classroom, she takes herself off with Holly, leaving Jem and me to our own devices.

'Bitch!' snarls Jem when he hears them laughing on the field one breaktime, some distance away. They're in the middle of a gang and they're having a good time. One by one people have drifted out into the sunshine but they join Megan and Holly, not us.

'They're not hurting you,' I say. I'm lying on my back trying to relax, but I'd much rather be having a laugh with the others. Jem's beginning to get on my nerves. It's not as if he's paying me any attention, he's too busy earwigging everyone else.

'Yes they are. They're offending me by their presence.'

Holly screeches at that moment at something someone says, as if to prove his point. I'm dying to know what they're laughing at.

'You don't know how pompous you sound,' I say, rolling over on to my belly and propping myself up on my elbows to watch them moodily. We're like a boring old married couple that nobody wants to talk to. I scramble to my feet. 'Come on! Let's go and join them!'

'No way.' Jem lies down flat on his back. The others notice I've got up and pause to watch me. What am I supposed to do now?

'Come on, Jem,' I plead quietly.

'You want to go and sit with them, go ahead,' says Jem, his eyes hidden by his sunglasses. 'But don't expect me to join you.'

I can feel the others staring. Darren says something to Holly and she giggles. I pull my band out of my hair and shake my hair loose defiantly. 'Right then, if that's the way you want it.'

When I go over to sit with them, Megan budges up to make room for me and puts her arm through mine. Not long after, the bell goes. When I get up to go back into school there's no sign of Jem.

At lunchtime he's nowhere to be seen so I go to the canteen with Megan. He's there already, sitting at a table by himself. We help ourselves to sandwiches and a glass of milk each, put them on trays and pay for them at the till. When I look up he's watching me and gives me a wave and I say, 'Come and sit with Jem?' and Megan looks a bit unsure but I insist, 'Please, Meg,' and she nods, so we make our way across the crowded canteen towards him. He sits up as we approach and smiles and pulls a chair out for Megan and I think, thank goodness for that, maybe, just maybe, we can all be friends at last. But the next minute I know, once and for all, there's just about as much chance of that happening as the Dag inviting Jem home for afternoon tea because Megan's tray flies up in the air and her milk splatters all over the place as she falls to the floor with a crash. The whole canteen cheers and applauds as Megan scrambles to her feet and screams, 'Bastard!' and slaps Jem loudly across the face.

He's pulled her chair away.

Then suddenly a hush falls and I look up to see Mr Davey standing before us.

'What the hell is going on here?' he thunders, taking in the whole scene with one glance.

'Your daughter attacked me.' Jem's voice is insolent, taunting. 'What you going to do about it?'

'Is this true?' Mr Davey asks Megan.

'Yes,' she snarls. 'Scum!'

The Assistant Head turns and appeals to everyone in the canteen. 'Did anyone see what took place here?' Suddenly everyone is intensely interested in their plates of chips and curled-up sandwiches.

'I did,' I say quietly.

Megan scowls at me. Jem grins. Mr Davey runs his hands through his hair and says, 'You'd better come along as well then. You two, my office. Now!'

I don't know what Jem thought I was going to do. Lie for him? He should have known better. It was his fault, not Megan's. It was a mean, spiteful thing to do, to whip her chair away like that. After I'd said my piece, Mr Davey went ballistic.

'You could have disabled her for life!' he bellows at Jem. 'Is that what you wanted?'

Of course he didn't. It was designed to humiliate, not harm; he's not a psychopath. He won't look at me. He's gazing out of the window as if he hasn't got a care in the world. Only I can tell from the set of his jaw that he's mad.

At me? Well, sorry, Jem, it's your own fault. You deserve to get done.

'And as for you . . .' Mr Davey turns his attention to

Megan. She looks really upset now and I don't blame her. It must be doubly humiliating to be bawled out of the canteen in front of the whole school by your own father. 'Did you have to retaliate? That's no way to settle your differences, with your fists.'

Satisfying though. I've been there. It's not Megan's style, however. She stares fixedly at her shoes, like if she stops concentrating for one minute she'll burst into tears. A heavy silence hangs over the room. It suddenly occurs to me that Mr Davey doesn't know what to do.

'It looks to me as if you're both to blame,' he says finally. 'Quite honestly I think you should apologize to each other and shake on it. There's nothing to be gained by taking this any further.'

Jem turns his head to look at him. 'No suspension this time? Not even a detention? Dear me, you are letting us off lightly, Sir. I wonder why that is?'

The Assistant Head's face turns purple. 'Don't push your luck, Jermaine. One more suspension and you're out of this school for good.'

Jem studies him coolly. 'In that case I think I'd better apologize to poor Megan, don't you? Sorry, Megan, for pulling your chair away and making you look a prat. I won't do it again. Ever.'

His tone is perfect, just the right side of insulting. His face is inscrutable.

At this moment I hate him.

'Megan?' Mr Davey looks as if he's keeping a firm hold on his temper. He's desperate to bring this to closure, you can tell. She grimaces.

'Sorry, Jem, for hitting you. I won't hurt you or anyone else again. Ever.'

Wow, Megan! Parodying Jem. Be careful. She means it though. And it's her father she's telling, not Jem.

Mr Davey looks relieved. 'Now get back to your classrooms and let's hope this is an end to all this nonsense. Kally, thank you for being such an honest witness.'

I nod. Outside the office Jem turns to me and says, 'Yeah, thanks, Kally,' but at this precise moment, I don't care. I shrug him off and follow Megan down the corridor.

After school he's waiting for me. He's leaning on the wall outside my classroom and when I come out he takes me by the arm and says, 'I want a word with you.'

'What?'

'Thanks for sticking up for me.'

'What do you expect? I saw you do it, everyone did.'

'Everyone else wasn't prepared to split on me though.'

'That's because they're scared of you. You don't frighten me, Jem.'

'No,' he says thoughtfully, 'I don't, do I?'

He doesn't seem mad and it throws me. I expected

him to be furious with me and I've been gearing myself up all afternoon for an almighty row. But it's weird; it's almost as if he admires me for what I did. I'm not sure I'm too proud of myself any more though, splitting on him like that. It's just at the time I thought it was a really mean thing to do and I didn't want Megan to get into trouble for slapping him one. I'd have done the same.

'Sorry.'

'Pardon?' He cups his hand behind his ear and leans towards me. 'I didn't hear that. Can you speak up?'

'Sorry for dobbing you in. Even if you did ask for it.'

''S'all right, no harm done.' He grins at me lazily. 'Funny though, wasn't it? Seeing her on the floor like that, covered in milk?'

I chuckle, more because I'm relieved he's forgiven me than the thought of Megan, but my timing is awful. Mr Davey goes past and glowers at us both. I know he's overheard us. Jem thinks it's hilarious, but my heart sinks. I don't know what it is, but being around Jem is just courting disaster.

Outside we mess about in the car park for a while on Jem's skateboard. We're not supposed to do this but since when has that stopped Jem doing anything? There's a nice piece of smooth tarmac, ideal to perfect my kick-flips. There's no easy way so I just keep on practising until at last, to my delight, I manage to land one on the move.

'Now I want you to repeat it a hundred times,' he says. Yeah, right. You're a hard taskmaster, Jem. But it's the least I can do to put things right between us. Every so often he yells at me to watch out as the staff leave in their cars, grumbling at us to get out of their way. I'm so engrossed in what I'm doing, I take no notice. And that's how I nearly get myself killed.

Mr Davey's my would-be assassin of all people. He's not parked with the others, you see, in the car park. He's got his own space next to the ones marked Head and Chairman of Governors and he zooms off down the drive after a particularly stressful day at work, safe in the knowledge that all his errant charges will be off the premises by now and safely home with their adoring parents.

Wrong. Out of the car park one appears in full flight, head down, knees bent to absorb the landing, totally oblivious to the fact that she's about to be wiped out by a deadly heap of metal with much bigger wheels and a 2000 cc engine. Just in time, Jem yells, 'KALLEEEE . . . !!!!!' and I look up and dive out of the way, somehow avoiding obliteration by centimetres. The board shoots ahead. There's a screeching of brakes and a clunking, clashing, cracking sound as the car slams to a stop and Mr Davey, white-faced, jumps out.

'You all right?'

I nod and accept his hand to pull myself up. I'm

covered in dirt and gravel but there are no bones broken, thanks to Jem.

Jem. Where is he?

He's standing by the car, staring in horror at his beloved board which is caught under the wheels. Even from here I can see a mangled deck and twisted trucks. It's a wreck.

'Shit!' says Mr Davey and bends down to try to disentangle the wreckage. He runs his hand over his nearside wheel. The tyre is going down before our eyes with a loud hissing sound and the wheel trim is hanging off. 'What a mess.'

'It's all my fault!' I wail. 'I'm sorry, Jem!'

'Sorry, Jem! What about my car!' mutters Mr Davey. He turns to Jem. 'You know you're not allowed to skate at school! See what happens when you insist on breaking the rules?'

Jem, white-faced and stricken, looks like he's in a trance but his eyes flicker towards the teacher. 'My fault, is it?'

'Skating in the car park! She could have been killed! That could have been Kally under those wheels!'

'Yeah and it would have been if I hadn't yelled to her to get out of your way. You should look where you're going!'

Mr Davey looks chastened. 'Well, at least it's just the

skateboard that got damaged. Plus my car.'

'*Just* the skateboard?' Jem's voice is deadly quiet.

Jem's beautiful, customized, unique board, each wheel, truck, bolt and bearing lovingly chosen, assembled and maintained to perfection by him. It's his pride and joy; he loves and cherishes it more than anything in the world. Or anyone. I suddenly have a terrible thought. Would he prefer it to be me lying there under those wheels, damaged beyond repair? My blood runs cold.

He thrusts his hands in his pockets as if he doesn't trust himself to keep them away from making contact with the teacher's face and without warning starts walking down the drive away from us.

'Jem!' calls Mr Davey. 'Come back here!'

Jem ignores him and strides on towards the gate.

'Jem!' I shout. 'What about your skateboard?'

'Bin it,' he yells back over his shoulder. 'That's all it's good for now.'

Mum's feeling down again. When I get home from school that night, feeling pretty shaky I don't mind admitting, and looking forward to a bit of TLC myself, I find out she's taken herself off to bed with a migraine (I thought those had disappeared) and Izzy has appointed herself in charge of tea. ('It's a surprise for Mum!')

Standing on a chair at the worktop, clad in one of my favourite tops ('Look, Kally, I remembered to cover up my school uniform!'), she's busy adding the finishing touches of dollops of brown sauce to a plate of chocolate biscuits heaped high with cold baked beans. ('I opened the tin myself. My first time!')

I try to ignore the streaks of bean juice adorning the delicate fabric of my pretty cream halter-neck ('It's like a pinny, isn't it?') and make a tactful suggestion. 'Shouldn't baked beans be hot, Iz?'

She rolls her eyes to heaven. 'I haven't finished yet,

have I?' She thrusts a spoon under my nose. 'Lick?' I decline the generous offer and watch spellbound as she clambers down, plate tipping dangerously to one side. One choccie biscuit, top heavy with its unfamiliar load, makes a bid for freedom and slides on to the floor, landing face down. Undeterred, Izzy picks it up and puts it back on the plate, scooping the baked beans off the floor and arranging them neatly on top. Then, domestic goddess that she is, she painstakingly wipes the baked beans clean of kitchen-floor grub with her fingers and bungs the whole lot in the microwave. And rubs her fingers clean on my best top.

'There,' she says with satisfaction, turning it up to High. 'Won't be long. I'll give Mum a call.'

Maybe it's Mum's migraine that makes her look queasy. She smiles valiantly when she sees the brown, sticky mess and says faintly, 'Izzy! How lovely!' but she doesn't seem to have much of an appetite. Me neither, but that's to be expected after my near-death experience. Never mind. Izzy tucks in for both of us.

Later, when Izzy's in bed and Mum had made us both some scrambled eggs, I find out what's really wrong with her.

Emma Preston has disappeared off the face of the earth. The chief witness.

'Did *she* do it then, Mum? Was it her all the time?'

Mum puts her plate to one side and stares gloomily into the hearth.

'It looks like it. The police want to interview her again, that's for sure.'

'How did they find out?'

'Well, it's Geoff we've got to thank really. He's an ex-policeman as you know, a detective. When I told him what had happened to your dad, he said it rang bells with a similar case he'd been involved with some years ago so he did a bit of investigating.'

'You told him?' I knew it. 'You said we mustn't let anyone know about Dad!'

'I know, Kally. I couldn't stand people gossiping. I didn't want you to go through all that again. A fresh start, that's what I wanted for you. But Geoff was different. I had to tell him because he was my employer and he believed me, he trusted me, from the start. And I knew he would be discreet.' She looks at me guiltily. 'I'm sorry, Kally. I know you haven't breathed a word to anyone.'

It's my turn to look guilty. Quickly I say, 'What I don't get about all this is, why didn't it all come out at the trial? Surely she would have been a suspect too.'

Mum bit her lip. 'Someone was shielding her.'

'Who?'

'Your father.'

⋆ ⋆ ⋆

I knew this would happen. Jem wants revenge on Mr Davey.

'He did it on purpose.' We're in the canteen, alone. Word's gone round what's happened and everyone's giving Jem a wide berth. This morning on the school bus, Darren yelled from the back, 'Sorry to hear about your board, mate,' and Jem told him to 'F*** off,' and the whole bus went silent. Now people are just staying out of his way, afraid of saying the wrong thing.

'Don't be daft, Jem. How could he? He didn't know I was going to come skating out of the car park at that precise moment.'

'Oh, he knew all right. He was biding his time, waiting to get his own back on me for upsetting his precious daughter's feelings.'

'You're being paranoid. He's not like that.'

Jem curls his lip. 'Oh yeah, I forgot. You're on her side.'

'No I'm not!'

He shrugs. He's the picture of despair, elbows on knees, head hanging down, gazing blindly at the floor. My heart goes out to him. I know how much that board meant to him. And he's never blamed me, not once. I lean forward and take his hand.

'I'm on your side, idiot.'

'Are you?'

'Of course I am.'

He's so good-looking when he's sad. With his eyes cast down like this, his eyelashes practically rest on his cheeks and his downturned mouth makes me want to kiss him, right here in the middle of the canteen, but I wouldn't do that.

He turns my hand over and traces the lines on my palm. It tickles. I must find out which is my love line. That long one hopefully. Or maybe the one that splits off near the base. Hmm.

'Then come round tonight and prove it.'

All I really want to do tonight is continue that conversation with Mum. Last night she clammed up after dropping her bombshell. Why would Dad cover up for Emma Preston to the extent that he was prepared to go to prison for her? Why would someone do a thing like that?

Because he was in love with her.

NO WAY!

Dad was in love with Mum, anyone could see that. OK, he might not have been all hearts and Valentines and red roses and slopping all over her, but they were too old for all that anyway.

So how can I be sure?

- Because he brought her a cup of tea in bed every day because Mum was not a morning person.

- Because as soon as he came in the house he would say, 'Where's your mother?'
- Because if she said, 'The kitchen's looking sad,' he'd buy a pot of paint and cheer it up for her.
- Because when she asked him if she was getting fat he'd shake his head and say, 'You're perfect,' even if she was looking like Mrs Blobby.
- Because he'd allow himself to be dragged along to rock'n'roll classes with her even though he had two left feet and football was on the telly.
- Because he'd buy her clothes for her birthday that were far too young and far too tight and then be surprised when they didn't fit and she'd have to take them back.
- Because he was.

But Mum had said too much already and anyway I had more pressing matters to attend to.

'I'm going out with Jem tonight, Mum, is that OK?'

'Where you going?'

'Pictures.' I lie without blushing. Bad sign. 'Can I have a bath?'

'Don't use all the hot water, Izzy needs one too. And don't be late, you've got . . .'

'School in the morning,' I finish for her and lock myself in the bathroom. I splash lashings of Mum's best bath oil in the water and fill it up to the brim. Oops, sorry, Izzy, I want to look my best tonight.

Afterwards I dress myself in my new vest top and favourite baggy jeans, decide to leave my hair down in a glorious orange frizz and spray myself in my Christmas perfume. I look at the result in the mirror. Not bad. Not bad at all.

By the time I get to Jem's house I'm not quite so laid-back. When I ring the doorbell my heart's thudding. Jem answers, thank goodness, looking cool as.

'Where's your gran?'

'Gran?' He looks nonplussed for a second then grins.

'Gone to bingo,' he explains. 'Should be out for an hour or two with a bit of luck. You look nice.' He bends to give me a kiss. 'Smell nice too.'

Nice! I smell gorgeous! I follow him upstairs and into his room. It's a mess. His bed is unmade with the duvet trailing on the floor and abandoned socks peeping from beneath. Stained mugs, half full of cold coffee, and empty crisp packets litter every available surface, while discarded clothing lies in heaps on the floor. Sorry, Jem, your walls may be a testament to your devotion to me but the rest of your room sucks! Something tells me I've got the wrong end of the stick and I feel a huge sense of relief and at the same time, paradoxically, let down. Gingerly, I remove a pair of boxers from a chair and sit down. He sits on the floor beside me.

'Go on then,' I say lightly. 'Give it to me. What have I got to do to prove I'm on your side?'

'I need your help.' He gazes at me steadily but there's a suppressed excitement about him that makes me uneasy. 'Are you up for it?'

''Course I am.' His mouth twists into a triumphant smile and I add quickly, 'If I can. Depends what you want me to do.'

His eyes gaze deeply into mine.

'If you really care about me, you'll do it.'

'Do what?'

'Help me get rid of Davey.'

I gasp.

'What do you mean, get rid of . . .?' For a mad moment I wonder if he's thinking of fixing his brakes or pushing him out of a second-floor window. Come on, Jem, I know you hate his guts and revenge is your second name, but it's your skateboard he wrote off, not your own mother. My horror must show in my face because Jem sniggers.

'Don't look so shocked, Kally. I'm not asking you to help me top him. I just want to get him the sack.'

'I knew you wouldn't.' Jem's gone into major sulk because I've refused to have anything to do with his crazy plan. I can't believe he would think up something so stupid. What the hell is going on in his head?

It's not just stupid. It's horrible. It's mean and spiteful and sordid and . . . weird. I don't like Jem when he's like this. It's like he's capable of anything.

'Kally, listen to me!' he persists when I go into shrieks of protest. 'It's the only way. It's dead hard for teachers to be sacked. It doesn't matter how crap they are, they still keep them on till they're so old they're drooling.'

'He's not crap. He's a good teacher.'

'He's a bullying bigot who hates my guts and wants to get rid of me. There's no room for both of us in that school, Kally. One of us is going, that's for sure. It's either him or me.'

I stare at Jem miserably. 'Not that way.'

'It's got to be. It's the one thing schools won't tolerate, teachers coming on to pupils. Please, Kally,' he grabs my arms, 'I'm begging you.'

I shrug him off. 'You're sick!'

'No, listen!' His voice is urgent. 'I'm not asking you to say he's done anything, just make out he's a bit too friendly. Then they'll have to have an investigation.'

'Read my lips! I'm not doing it!'

'All right then, just make an allegation, let him stew for a few days, then drop it. Say you got it wrong and no harm done. We'll just give the smug bastard a fright, yeah?'

I stare at him in disbelief. 'Why are you asking me to do this, Jem?'

He misunderstands. 'To prove how you feel,' he says simply.

That's not what I mean. But I know the real reason, anyway.

This is fighting Jem. The big I Am. Nobody pushes me around. Davey destroyed my skateboard so Davey's got it coming to him. Get mad. Get even.

'What about Megan? How's she going to feel?'

He shrugs. 'She'll get over it. It won't be for ever.'

'Get lost, Jem.'

★ ★ ★

He tries everything, sweet-talking, nagging, bullying, sulking, all the emotional blackmail you can think of, but like well-oiled wheels on new-laid tarmac, his words roll over me but leave an impression I can't get rid of. I'm irritated beyond belief. How can he be so self-obsessed?

'Jem, it's totally freaky what you're asking me to do!' He looks genuinely surprised at my outrage and this so infuriates me I practically spit with rage. 'I'm the last person who'd accuse someone of something they haven't done. I've been there, remember? I know what it feels like to have a father everyone points the finger at. And no, Jem, Megan wouldn't get over it, believe me.'

'OK, OK. Forget I ever mentioned it.' At last he's got the message. He looks really pissed off now. 'At least we know where we stand.'

'Meaning?'

'Nothing.' He studies me coolly. 'Anyway, there's more than one way to skin a cat.'

'Jem, what are you going on about?'

He ignores me. I'm no longer important. 'I'm going to get a drink.' He goes out, banging the door behind him as if he can't bear to be in the same room as me any more. Well, ditto. Soon he's crashing round in the kitchen and then his gran must have come in because I can hear them talking. It's obvious he's in no rush to be with me again; even her company's preferable to mine.

Should I go? I get up and prowl restlessly round his room, moodily examining the photos of me in happier times on the wall. I'm fed up with it all. It's no longer fifty/fifty. The cons of going out with Jem are definitely outweighing the pros. He's too random. I mean, what sort of guy would want to pull a trick like that?

The same sort of guy who plasters his walls top to toe with pictures of his girlfriend. Where are his skating posters showing tricks, decks, clothes, celebrities? Where's Charlie T?

Actually, I think they're behind the photos of me. Studying that first one he took of me all those months ago as I step off the school bus, face turned towards the camera, eyes wide in surprise, I notice a corner curling up to reveal another photograph beneath. I lean over to peer at it closely.

It's a girl. What's this, a rival? Or a previous girlfriend, more like, supplanted, obviously, by my superior qualities. What if she's better-looking than me? I can't resist removing the drawing pin in the top corner and gently peeling back my smiling face.

I gasp.

It's a photograph of Laura Baker. She's smiling into the camera too but there's no contest, I definitely win the beauty stakes here. She's got no eyes, you see. They've been stabbed out.

There are more. I tear my grinning, stupid, naive face off the wall to reveal other photographs of Laura, similarly defaced. Some of them have crude, vile words scrawled all over them. I rip them away blindly till my stomach churns and I feel sick.

'Kally?'

Jem stands in the doorway, his hand on the frame. He looks scared.

'Oh shit!' I can feel my hands cupped against my nose and mouth, pressing hard, but it's no good. I charge past Jem, pushing him out of the way, I swear, by the sheer force of my revulsion, and hurtle blindly down the stairs.

'What's going on?' says Mrs Smith, bewildered, coming out of the kitchen.

'Come back!' Jem yells, from the top of the stairs. 'Let me explain!'

'What have you done now!' shrieks his gran but I don't wait for him to explain. I'm too busy yanking open the front door and making it, just in time, to the gutter where I throw up the entire contents of my stomach in long, agonizing convulsions of disgust and I don't stop until there is nothing left. Nothing at all.

It's over. You don't need me to tell you that. He never loved me. He was just using me to get at Laura. All that business about picking up Izzy. I thought he was doing it for me.

It's OK, Kal. You go to netball practice and I'll pick up Izzy.

How could I be so stupid? It was just an excuse to see Laura. She didn't want to know but he wouldn't leave her alone.

So many things fall into place now. I'll never forget her frightened face and that cold, clear little voice, full of bravado, protesting,

I've told you before, you're not to come into this classroom. You've no right. I'll get the caretaker if necessary.

I went home after I'd thrown up. I remember Jem pleading with me, begging me to stop and talk to him. I was crying. He was too. I yelled, 'I hate you, leave me alone!' and I ran off. All the way home he kept ringing me and I wouldn't answer but in the end I did.

'We're finished.'

'You said you'd never leave me!'

'I've changed my mind.' My voice cracks. 'You're weird, Jem. You need help.'

There's a silence at the other end. Then he says quietly, 'Bitch.'

I drop my phone as if it's toxic and stamp on it. Then I kick the bits into the hedge.

I feel as if I've been blasted in the face by the cold water of common sense. I'm in shock but it's cleansed my eyes. I'm seeing things crystal clear for the first time in ages.

You never had your phone pinched, did you, Jem? That was just another lie. I think deep down I knew all along it was you who pulled that mean stunt on the Dag, I just didn't want to believe it. And it wasn't for me, like you made out, it was so you could see Laura who hated your guts by then. All that other stuff too, Darren's board, Matt's bike, Holly's photo, Megan ending up on the floor, how could you be so cruel? It's like if you don't get your own way you turn into devil-boy and cause chaos. Now it's Mr Davey whose life you want to devastate. Well, I'm not going to let you.

I've been such an idiot.

At home I try to sneak upstairs but Mum catches me and takes one look at my face and says, 'What's happened?' and I burst into tears. We go into the sitting room and she wraps her arms round me until I stop sobbing, then she says worriedly, 'Jem hasn't done anything he shouldn't, has he?' and daft as it sounds, I chuckle, because I can tell by her face what she's thinking. Why is it mums think the worst things boys can do is have sex with you? So I say, 'No, Mum, of course he hasn't,' which is quite absurd when you think about it because Jem has done millions of things he shouldn't have but he's never tried that, and she looks relieved and says, 'Just a row then. I thought as much.'

'No, Mum, it's more than that, I've broken up with him.'

She puts on a wise, understanding face and pats my hand. 'What you need is a good night's sleep. It'll all seem better in the morning.'

I could hit her for being so naive. But then I am too, so it must be a family trait.

Needless to say, I lie awake all night, tossing and turning. I'm hurt beyond belief. He told me he loved me and I believed him. But he's not capable of loving anyone, is he? He just wants to control them. Then I start getting scared. What if he picks on *me* now? What if he starts following me round like he did Laura? I start shaking. Jem will want revenge, that's for sure. Well, I'm just going to have to be strong.

Mr Davey knows about him. He tried to warn me off. If only I'd listened. Suddenly, like a bolt out of the blue, I know for certain that this has happened before.

Jem's not behaving as I expected him to. Why does that surprise me? I guess I should have foreseen it. His unpredictability is predictable.

Mum's wrong by the way. I don't feel better the next morning.

I get on the bus, tired and wrung-out like an old dishcloth, dreading the moment we get to his bus stop, but he's not there and I breathe a sigh of relief. As soon as I get to school I tell Megan it's over, determined that Jem won't get to me first. She gives me a hug and looks pleased but tactfully she refrains from asking me why. Not so, Holly.

'The rat! Did he try it on then dump you when you said no? Men, they're all the same!'

'It wasn't like that,' I remonstrate but she's not listening. By lunchtime it's all around the school that Jem's dumped me and to be honest I don't care. Let people say what they like; I'd rather them think I'm Jem's reject than find out the real reason we split up. People are nice. I get lots of hugs from the girls and gruff 'All rights?' from the boys.

Even Darren whispers in my ear, 'You were wasted on him anyway,' and then jumps back guiltily in case Jem is earwigging. But Jem is nowhere to be seen.

I consider going to Mr Davey and telling him everything but something stops me. I can't split on Jem like that. Anyway, he'd deny it.

As the days pass and there's still no sign of him, I start to wonder what all the panic was about. Gradually I move from relief to curiosity to concern about his whereabouts. Well, you can't just switch off your feelings, can you, especially when you've been glued to someone's hip for the past few months? He seems to have vanished off the face of the earth.

The trouble is, the longer it goes on, the more I think maybe I acted too hastily. When I'm in bed at night, I stop reminding myself that his behaviour was seriously scary and convince myself he's done something daft out of unrequited love for me, like string himself up from the nearest tree. But he'd have been found by now.

How do you do this, Jem? You're messing with my head and you're not even around. Ironic or what? There was me, scared he was going to stalk me, but instead he's vanished from my life without a trace and it's starting to really get to me. If this goes on much longer I'm going to have to talk to Megan about it. Maybe her dad knows where he is.

Mum's not much help either. After her initial sympathy she quickly loses interest. 'Not back together then?' she asks the next day when I get home from school and when I shake my head she adds, 'Ah well, perhaps it's just as well. You're too young to get serious.' Thanks a bunch, Mum. Subject closed. But then she adds, 'Plenty more fish in the sea,' and, 'Put it down to experience,' and I take myself off before she builds a wall of clichés between us.

The thing is she's got her own problems. She's preoccupied with Dad and the possibility of a retrial and she spends loads of time in the phone box talking to lawyers.

'They've really built up a case against that woman,' she says on Saturday, out of the blue, when we're washing up in the kitchen. Izzy's busy at the table operating. It's a revolutionary new procedure. She's taken the head off Ken (the organ donor) and is carefully removing his liver (a Jelly Tot) with a pair of tweezers. Other body parts (a button, a hook and eye, a paper clip, a Smartie) have already been extracted and are awaiting transplantation into Barbie who has already been decapitated, ready to receive her mutiple organ donation, her head lying composedly beside her. All seems to be going well but it's tricky and requires intense concentration from the surgeon so Mum obviously feels she's OK to talk without Izzy eavedropping, though she's careful not to mention names. 'It seems it's not the first time she's been involved in this sort of thing.'

'Why don't they just let him go?'

'They need to question her first. The thing is,' she nods meaningfully towards Izzy who's totally oblivious to our conversation, 'E. P. wasn't her real name and now she's vanished without a trace. But they'll find her, don't you fret.'

'Why did he cover up for her in the first place?'

'Misguided loyalties.'

'To her?'

'No, to me.'

I stare at her bemused. 'I don't get it.'

There's a knock on the front door. She throws the tea towel down with a sigh and goes to answer it. 'Neither did I, at first. I'll explain it all to you one day.'

I turn the radio on and start stacking the clean dishes back on the shelf. Izzy gives a shout of pleasure and I turn to see who's arrived. Jem stands uncertainly in the doorway, holding a bunch of orange and yellow flowers. Izzy launches herself at him and hugs him round the waist. He's wearing baggy blue jeans, layers of T-shirts and a baseball cap and he looks so cool.

Behind him Mum beams from ear to ear.

'These are for you.' He thrusts them into my hands.

My first bunch of flowers. (Not counting the ones Jem stole from the graveyard!) I don't know what I'm supposed to do with them.

'Where've you been?'

'Oh, you know . . .' he shrugs. Jem, lost for words? 'Can we talk?'

Mum springs into action. 'Come on, Izzy, we need to go shopping.'

'Mu-um! I want to see Jem. Lovely Jem.' Izzy snuggles closer to him.

'Shame. I was going to call in at the newsagent's, pick up a comic on the way back, perhaps a few sweets . . .'

'I'll come. Wait for me!' Izzy disappears and the front door slams.

Jem laughs. 'Bribery, eh?'

'Works every time.'

'Maybe we're all corrupt.' His smile fades. 'Kally, I'm sorry. I've been so stupid. Can you ever forgive me?' His face is open and pleading.

I hesitate. Come on, Kally, don't be stupid. This guy is dangerous, he's a time bomb waiting to go off. You've learned your lesson.

'It's over, Jem.'

'I know that, I know. I screwed up big-time. But I owe you an explanation at least. I won't try to persuade you to come back to me, I know you won't do that, but I just want you to know why I acted the way I did.'

'I don't know . . .'

'Please, Kally.'

I bite my bottom lip, considering. Everyone deserves a chance to explain. Maybe if Dad had explained what really happened, he wouldn't have ended up in prison. Now I've arrested, charged and proclaimed Jem guilty without even having heard his defence.

'OK then. But it won't make any difference.'

It did though. It made all the difference in the world. I always got the impression that Jem's real mother was at the root of his problems but I had no idea how completely dysfunctional she really was. We're talking serious issues here, a continuous cycle all through his life of neglect, rejection and abandonment followed by remorse and compensatory overindulgence, until boredom set in and it started all over again.

'For years she'd disappear from my life altogether, when some new bloke came on the scene. Or she'd get some crazy new get-rich-quick scheme in her head and that would be the last I'd see of her for months till she'd come back with her tail between her legs and whisk me away from wherever she'd left me.'

'Where did she get to?'

'All over the place. Sometimes she'd get a job and it

would be all right for a while then she'd screw up big-time. Or she'd shack up with someone but it never lasted. I reckon she's spent some time inside for fraud and theft too.'

'Poor you.' I grimace, knowing what it's like to have a parent in prison, though at least my dad was innocent. No wonder Jem kept it all bottled up inside. 'You must hate her for messing you about.'

'No.' He looks perplexed. 'That's the strange thing, I don't. But I find it really hard to trust anyone, women in particular. I always feel they're going to leave me eventually.'

I shift uncomfortably and he smiles ruefully.

'I'm not getting at you, Kally, but it's true. Everyone abandons me and I find it really hard to handle. I get really angry and I want to hit back. That's why I did those stupid things to Laura. I thought she liked me you see, but she didn't in the end. Nobody does.'

'I did! I do.'

Jem's face lights up and I add hastily, 'But this doesn't change anything, Jem. It's still over between us.'

He sighs. 'I know. I blew it, didn't I? But I just want you to know you've got nothing to be afraid of from me. I'd never hurt you.'

I give his arm a squeeze. 'She can't be that bad a mum. You're all right underneath.'

'D'you reckon?' His mouth twists into a half-smile. 'I'm proud of her in some ways. She's dead young and pretty. I get my good looks from her.' The smile expands into a wide grin and I have to remind myself firmly that I am no longer going out with this gorgeous guy.

'Do you want to see a photo?' To my surprise, Jem pulls his wallet out of his back pocket.

'Yeah, I'd love to!'

He rifles round in the back and takes out a small black and white photograph and hands it to me.

'What do you think? Pretty special, isn't she?'

My breath implodes. She's pretty special all right. I am looking at a head-and-shoulders photograph of a smart, youngish woman, carefully made up, long blonde hair escaping attractively from jewelled clips.

It's Emma Preston.

'THIS IS YOUR MUM?'

'Yeah. What d'you think?'

I don't know what to think! My head's racing. Emma Preston, Jem's mum? It can't be true. But then they say truth is stranger than fiction, the papers are full of it.

'Kally?' Jem's staring at me curiously. 'Are you OK?'

I swallow. 'Yeah, yeah. She's . . . very attractive. But . . .' something flickers inside me, a tiny flame of hope already doomed to die because he told me before he doesn't know where she is, 'it's a shame you're not in touch with her.'

He smiles. 'I am now. That's where I've been for the past week. I got a message from her out of the blue and I've been to see her.'

The tiny flame combusts into life. 'Where?'

'London.'

'Big place.' My mind shoots off in all directions. I don't know which way to go. Tell Mum? Tell Jem? Tell the police?

'Big enough to lose yourself in.' He snorts. 'She's been up to her old tricks again. Fraud. No surprises there. Some poor sod's in prison taking the flak for her so she's lying low till it all blows over.'

That 'poor sod' was my father. And *she*, Emma Preston, was intending to hide 'till it all blew over' and he'd served his time. *Her* time. I think I'm going to explode.

'She's evil!'

Jem looks at me in surprise. 'No she's not. She's got a conscience, somewhere deep down, believe it or not. She feels bad about it, she really does. She liked the guy.'

'Not enough to turn herself in though?'

'No, probably not.' His mouth twists into a bitter, resigned smile. 'Not unless there was something in it for her.'

The flames of hope are now leaping out of control and have turned into a raging, angry inferno.

'You don't get it, do you?'

'What?' Jem stares at me blankly.

'It's my dad you're talking about! Your mother passed herself off as Emma Preston!'

Jem's mouth hangs open with shock. 'You're joking?'

I shake my head. 'Like I'd joke about a thing like that! It's her, Jem. I recognized her straight away from that photo.'

'Oh shit!' He snatches the photograph from my fingers and stares at it as if he can't believe it. 'Mum, what the hell have you done this time?' He raises his head. 'What are you going to do?'

I take a deep breath. 'Tell the police, of course. It's the only thing I can do.'

He looks horrified. OK, I'm not comfortable with this either: I mean it's not exactly a good place to be, telling your ex that you're about to inform on his own mother, but I'm resolute. A huge injustice has been done and my dad's freedom is at stake. He stares back down at the picture, considering. At last, he nods as if he's reached a decision.

'You're right. But there may be another way.'

'What?' My tone is short. You're not going to wriggle out of this one, Jermaine Smith.

'I'll persuade her to confess instead. That way they may go a bit easier on her.'

I can't believe I'm hearing this. I feel as if I'm trapped inside a bad cops and robbers film. And excuse me, Jem, why would I want the police or the Crown Prosecution Service or anybody else for that matter to 'go easy' on your evil mother?

'Please, Kally. I think I can do it. And if you put the police on to her, she's only going to deny it all, isn't she, like she did before?'

And then it'll go on and on and all the time Dad will be festering away in prison and Mum will be pining away for him. He has a point.

'You reckon she'll tell the truth?'

He nods eagerly. 'She will if you come with me! Tell her what you told me, say what it's been like for your family. Let her hear it straight from the horse's mouth.'

'Me, go to London?'

'Yes, it's the best way. She's feeling bad about it anyway and if she thinks the game's up then I'm sure she'll go to the police herself and make a clean breast of it . . .'

He's speaking like he's inside that B-movie again, he must be upset. It is his mum after all.

'OK.'

He stands up. 'Come on then, let's go.'

'What, now?'

'What are you waiting for?'

'What about Mum?'

'Leave a note for her. Say you're staying over at Megan's for the night.'

'I don't know . . .'

'Look, if we get a move on, we can get a train to London this afternoon. We'll be back this time tomorrow. Think what brilliant news you'll have to tell your mum!'

'I don't think I've got enough money . . .'

'I've got plenty for both of us. Come on, Kally, we'll miss that train!'

I scribble a note for Mum and grab my bag before I

have time to change my mind. 'This is so good of you, Jem. I can't begin to tell you what this means to me.'

'Kally,' he says, his face serious, 'I owe you. This is the least I can do.'

We get as far as the end of the lane and see Izzy hanging about outside the phone box, drawing wide sweeping circles in the dust with the toe of her shoe. Inside I can see Mum having an animated discussion on the phone. I can't make out if she's laughing or crying. She must be talking to Dad.

'Where you going?' asks Iz, wrapping her arms around us both and peering up at us, head back.

'Megan's.'

'Can I come?'

Mum spots us and raps on the side of the phone box. Her eyes are shining. She's happy. I give her a wave.

'Come on, Kally, we'll be late,' says Jem impatiently, disentangling himself from Izzy's embrace and turning away.

'No, Iz, not this time.' Her face falls. Impulsively I pick her up and hug her tight, burying my nose in her untidy hair. She smells of sweets. 'I love you,' I mumble.

'Love you more,' she responds, squeezing me round the neck till I can hardly breathe.

'Love you most,' I croak. She smiles at the familiar routine.

'Kally, we're going to miss that train!' hisses Jem. I put Izzy down and run to catch him up. When I look back, Izzy is standing alone by the phone box, a forlorn little figure. She raises her hand and waves in that baby way she still has, her small fist opening and closing, and I wave back with a lump in my throat, then, as I see Mum emerging from the box, I turn round and leg it after Jem.

We get to the station with seconds to spare. The guard's already standing by his van with his whistle between his teeth and a flag in his hand. When he sees us running up the platform, he holds a door open for us and bundles us in, then he blows his whistle and waves his flag and jumps in after us. The train pulls out and we charge down the carriage, collapsing laughing into the nearest empty seats, our chests heaving. We're on our way!

I sit back and watch buildings, roads and back gardens giving way to green fields and get my breath back. I must be mad! What will Mum think when she reads my note? Will she ring Megan's house to check up on me? No, of course not, why would she? Stop panicking, Kally. If this is what it takes to get Dad free, then do it!

Across from me, Jem delves into the depths of his rucksack and pulls out two chocolate bars and a couple of cans of fizzy drink. I'm starting to enjoy this. We munch companionably for a while and talk about what we're going to do when we get to London.

'It's easy,' says Jem confidently. 'Just a few stops on the Tube. I didn't expect to be going back there so soon.'

'Are you going to let her know we're coming?' I ask, suddenly daunted at the thought of confronting Emma Preston after all this time.

'Nope,' he says. 'Better to take her by surprise. Don't worry, it'll be fine, trust me.'

He grins at me reassuringly and I smile and relax back against the seat. Jem has everything under control as usual. After a while he takes out his iPod and puts on his headphones. He's so organized! I should have brought a book to read. But then, I didn't know, did I? Soon he's into his music and his eyes gradually take on a glassy, unfocused gaze before finally closing. His head drops. He's fast asleep. Thanks Jem, you're great company!

Bored, I lean over to reach for a newspaper on the empty seat across the aisle. It's an evening newspaper, a London edition, presumably abandoned by a commuter on their journey last night out of the capital. I glance through it, mildly interested. It's the one Dad used to get on his way home from work when we lived in London. I freeze.

I'm staring at a picture of Emma Preston surrounded by policemen. And the headline above says, in big, bold capitals,

WOMAN ARRESTED IN SKATE-PARK FRAUD.

My head goes into a spin. I need to wake Jem up and tell him we're on a wasted journey. His mother's already been arrested. Poor Jem, he can't make it easier for her, it's too late. All his plans have come to nothing.

All his plans . . . *Jem has everything under control as usual.* Two Cokes, two Mars bars, my favourite. *He's so organized.* He even brought his iPod with him to while away the time on the long journey to London.

'Tickets please!' It's the guard again. Jem wakes up with a jump and fishes round in his back pocket. He pulls out two tickets and gives them to the guard who zaps them in his machine and hands them back. Jem grins at me. 'All right?'

I nod and fold the paper up neatly and return it to the seat across the aisle, then stand up. 'I need the loo.'

What I really need is to sort out the crazy thoughts that are pulsating through my head and I can't do this with Jem sitting opposite me. I make my way down the aisle and into the door marked Vacant, bolting it behind me. Then I put the loo seat down and sit down on it. I need to think.

We nearly missed this train. If we hadn't jumped on it straight away it would have gone without us. We didn't have time to stop and buy tickets. If I'd thought about it I'd have assumed we would have bought them on the train.

But I didn't think. I haven't been thinking at all. Because if I had, I would have realized Jem had prepared for this journey very thoroughly. He'd brought the Cokes and the chocolate and the iPod and the tickets with him.

He knew we were going to London. He had it all planned.

Why?

The train slows down. We're pulling into a station. I turn the tap on and wash my hands then splash cold water over my face. The train stops with a jerk and I nearly miss my footing. Nearly. I pull the roller towel down and wipe my face and hands. That's better. Stay cool, Kally. With Jem you always have to be one trick ahead. Well, what's required of you now is nothing fancy; just a basic 180-degree turn. A shove-it.

When I unlock the toilet door and look down the carriage, I can see Jem's long legs stretched out into the aisle. He's closed his eyes again. I turn the other way towards the external door, pull down the window and reach outside for the handle. Then, as the train jerks into motion again, I step down on to the platform and walk quickly away.

I'm lucky. On the other side of the platform is a train going back down the line. I jump on, slump into a seat and pray that the ticket collector doesn't appear. Actually, that's the least of my worries.

The train lurches into action and slowly picks up speed. I stare out of the window but I don't register a thing. My heart is thudding and my mind is whirling with crazy, mixed-up thoughts. Jem's up to something and I don't get it and I'm scared stiff.

Don't panic, Kally. Just take a deep breath and calm down and go through it slowly, step by step.

Fact. He must have known already that his mother was Emma Preston.

Question. When did he find out?

Answer. He put two and two together, I suppose, when I

told him about her and the scheming role she'd played in my dad's downfall. Huh! I should have kept my mouth shut like Mum told me to.

I stiffen. Maybe he knew before that? There was that time when I came home from netball practice and he was in my bedroom, looking after Izzy. I remember spotting my diary next to him and being uneasy. I was afraid he'd had a look and found out how much I liked him. But there was all that stuff about Dad in there too.

Scary.

Question. In that case, why did he pretend he didn't know?

Answer. Stop being paranoid, Kally. Use your common sense. Probably his mum told him this week. He'd been up to see her, remember? He only came home yesterday.

But hang on. In that case she must have been arrested while he was up there. It was splashed all over last night's London evening newspaper, for goodness' sake. So . . .

Question. What was the point of this wild-goose chase anyway?

My head's going round in circles. None of this makes sense. If only he hadn't shown me that photograph in his wallet in the first place, none of this would have happened.

Suddenly, like a bolt out of the blue, it hits me. I groan out loud. How could I be so stupid?

That photograph. It was the same one. It was the one from last night's paper, only the background had been wiped out and it had been reduced to a head-and-shoulders shot. He must have done it on his computer when he got back from London last night. Easy-peasy stuff for Jem, the great photographer.

Fact. His mother wasn't Emma Preston at all. He just pretended she was.

Question. Why?

Answer. So you'd go away with him.

Oh no, this is weird. What the hell did he have in mind?

I owe you.

He owes me all right. Big-time. If you don't do what Jem wants you to, he gets revenge.

Jem, my dark boy, what devious designs did you have on me?

When I step off the train I have a welcoming committee. There's a crowd on the platform, Mum and Izzy, Geoff, Mr Davey and Megan, Jem's gran, they're all here together. Like, why?

The funny thing is, no one notices me, they're too

busy cross-examining the poor station manager who is thumbing through a timetable and looking rather fraught. Suddenly Izzy looks up and yells, 'Kally!' and dashes up the platform to take me out in her favourite waist-high tackle, with Mum in hot pursuit behind her.

'We thought you'd run away with Jem,' Izzy explains. 'Can I come next time?'

I can't talk. Mum's flung her arms around me and is squeezing me so tight I can't breathe. She's repeating, 'Oh thank goodness you're all right, thank goodness,' and tears are running down her cheeks and when she finally lets me go, Megan strangles me with a hug too.

Then Mr Davey says, 'Where is he?' and I answer, 'On the train to London,' because there's no point in lying and I have no reason whatsoever to protect Jem any more. And Geoff says, 'We'll have him when he gets into Paddington,' and takes out his mobile.

'What ever were you thinking of?' snaps Mum, between mopping up her tears.

'I wasn't running away, Mum. We were going to see someone who I thought could help me free Dad.'

Mum stares at me blankly. 'Who?'

I glance sideways at Jem's gran, feeling suddenly awkward. 'Jem's real mother.'

'What?' Mrs Smith's face wrinkles up into a puzzled frown. 'What do you mean? *I'm* Jem's real mother.'

He'd lied about that too. Was there anything Jem hadn't lied about? His one saving grace in my eyes had been that he couldn't help it, he was a product of his dysfunctional childhood. I mean, if you've been repeatedly rejected by your own mother, then you'd expect to have a few issues to deal with, wouldn't you?

Only he hadn't. Been rejected I mean. He certainly had plenty of issues. He'd made it all up. His long-suffering mum had always been there for her miscreant son, through every single trick he'd ever pulled. And there had been lots of them.

'His bloody gran!' Mrs Smith explodes. 'Bloody cheek!' Izzy's face lights up and I see her lips moving as she repeats Mrs Smith's words with quiet satisfaction. 'I just don't know what to do with him, Mr Davey. He's a law unto himself.'

There then follows a lengthy catalogue of Jem's

misdemeanours, all brought on by her indignation at finding out her son had passed her off to me as his grandmother. They're pretty formidable and I notice Mum visibly blanching. 'I thought he was such a nice boy,' she mutters. I look at Mr Davey miserably, half expecting him to say, 'I told you so,' but all he does is give me a wry smile. Megan's hand steals into mine and I squeeze it gratefully.

Mr Davey jumps into authority-mode. 'The important thing is to find him. Is there anywhere he'd be likely to head for in London?'

Mrs Smith shrugs. 'There's my sister's. That's where he's been for the past week. He's been down since he and Kally quarrelled so I suggested he went there for a bit of a break. He was very cut up, you know, love, when you split up. He's not all bad.'

I know that. It would be so much easier if he was.

'Don't worry.' Mr Davey pats her arm. 'He'll turn up.'

'Like a bad penny,' says Mrs Smith miserably. 'Let's hope so.'

But I'm not sure she means it.

That night after Izzy has gone to bed, I sit up and talk to Mum.

'I'm sorry, Mum.'

'It wasn't your fault. Oh, if I could get my hands on

that boy . . .' Mum's face contorts with fury as she plans how she'd like to get even with Mr Nasty. I sigh heavily.

'How did you know I'd gone off with him anyway?'

'I didn't at first. I read your note and thought you were at Megan's. Then Geoff came round with some good news and I couldn't wait to tell you so I rang Megan's from his phone. Her dad answered and told me you weren't there. I knew then you'd gone off with Jem. I was out of my mind with worry.'

I bite my lip in remorse. 'It's not like you thought. I wasn't planning to spend the night with him or anything. I just wanted to sort things out for Dad. Anyway,' a thought strikes me, 'how come you knew we'd got on a train?'

'Izzy said Jem told you to hurry up or you'd miss it.'

I chuckle. 'She doesn't miss a trick, does she?'

'So Mr Davey went to get Jem's mother,' continues Mum, 'and they met us at the station. Anyway, we had no idea where you'd gone; we were looking to see which trains had gone out when you appeared.' She shudders. 'I never want to go through that again.'

I swallow. 'I've been so stupid, haven't I? Believing him like that.'

She pulls me to her and gives me a hug. 'We all make mistakes.' I lie still for a while in the safety of her arms, my face against her breast, feeling it rise and fall to her regular breathing.

'Mum? Emma Preston or whatever her real name is? What was it all about?'

She's silent for a moment. Then she starts explaining in a calm, even tone, as if she's finally come to terms with what happened.

'She was out to set him up from the start. She was going to raise the money then disappear with it, that was always her intention. But they got on so well, you know your dad, he gets on with everyone, and she didn't bargain on that. She wanted him to go with her.'

'Dad?' I sit up and stare at Mum in horror.

'Yes. She had a crush on him, you see. And your dad was too dim to realize. When she told him what she wanted, he was scared stiff! He told her to get on her bike and leave him alone!' She snorted derisively. 'Not a good idea. That's when she got nasty.'

'What do you mean?'

'She pinched the money anyway, then said she would tell me they'd been having an affair if he told the police it was her.'

'You wouldn't have believed that, would you, Mum?'

She pauses.

'I don't know. You can believe anything if someone's convincing enough.'

I nod slowly. I know that now.

'She convinced your father anyway. I always had my doubts about her, everyone did. I thought it would all come out at the trial. But when he was asked if there was any reason he thought Emma Preston could be responsible for the money disappearing, he looked straight at her and said, "No." He lied to save our marriage and went to prison for it.'

'Poor Dad.' I smile up at her. 'His motives were good.'

'The path to hell is paved with good intentions,' intones Mum morosely. We lie there together on the sofa, arms draped round each other, lost in our own thoughts. Then I remember.

'Anyway, what was it?'

'What?'

'The reason you rang Megan? The good news you had to tell me?'

Mum's face breaks into a wide smile.

'Your father's coming home.'

Mr Davey was wrong for once. Jem managed to avoid the police at Paddington and he never got to his aunt's. Nobody knows where he is, no one in school anyway. Megan thinks Mrs Smith does and she's shielding him. Mum reckons she knows he's safe somewhere.

'Maybe she just doesn't care?' I say to Mum.

'She didn't strike me like that,' she says shortly. 'He's her own son, where all's said and done. Poor soul, she's got her hands full with that one.'

It turns out Jem's got history. He's been in trouble all his life. He was kicked out of his last school for pestering a young female teacher. Sound familiar? His mum brought him down here and rented a house for a fresh start, just like mine did. But your past has a way of catching up with you.

Mr Davey knew this. He tried to warn me. But I wouldn't listen.

Within days, Mrs Smith has done a bunk. I walk past Jem's house. It's empty, no neat curtains, no plant in the window, no loud music belting out from upstairs. It's as if he's never been there. Did I imagine it all?

'Gone to join her son,' says Mr Davey. 'Silly woman, she's doing him no favours, shielding him like that. He's a nasty piece of work.'

But he's wrong again. In a way. It's not as simple as that. I've been thinking about it a lot. Tonight I'm in my favourite position, kneeling on the floor by my open bedroom window, arms draped over the sill, with the cool night air wafting in. In the field opposite, the cows stand close together for warmth, their shapes solid and bulky under the night sky. It's a new moon.

Behind me, Izzy is reciting nursery rhymes tonelessly. She's got stuck in the groove of 'Three Blind Mice'. She loves the bit with the tails and the carving knife.

I'm lost in my own thoughts, struggling to understand the enigma that was Jem. What was his plan?

He could be evil, that's for sure. He was the stuff of nightmares, obsessive, ruthless, vindictive.

But he could be good too. He was a person of extremes and contradictions. I don't know what he had in mind, dragging me off to London like that under false pretences, but I know one thing for definite. He'd never have hurt me. And he loved Izzy. That was genuine.

She's moved on from the luckless mice at last. She's reciting the strange tale of the little girl with the little curl in the middle of her forehead. I turn round and smile at her and join in the last lines, deliberately changing the pronoun.

> '*When he was good, he was very, very, good.*
> *But when he was bad, he was horrid.*'

She giggles. 'You got it wrong, Kally!'

'I did, didn't I?' Out of the mouths of babes and innocents. I hold out my hand to her and she scampers out of bed to join me at the windowsill, leaning her small chin on her hands, like a little squirrel.

'Who's that?'

I follow her gaze and go rigid. A figure is standing at the garden gate. My eyes close with shock.

Déjà vu. Day Sha Voo.

Was it you all those months ago, that lone figure at the gate? Jem, have you returned to haunt me?

Automatically my arm searches for Izzy's warm little body and I pull her close to me, protectively. Suddenly she leaps up and screeches. He's opened the gate and is coming up our garden path.

'IT'S HIM!' she yells. 'KALLY, IT'S DAD!'

Sometimes I think I see him. Long dark hair crammed under a black beanie, layers of T-shirts, low-slung baggy jeans. He's skating, hard and fast, in his concentrated, self-absorbed way, repeating each trick till he nails it perfectly. My heart misses a beat . . .

Once I dreamt I saw him with a girl and I thought, poor thing, she doesn't have a clue what she's letting herself in for.

But in that confused, shadowy, halfway state between sleeping and wakening, I clung to my dream, wishing it were me.